TAKEN BY THE ELDERMAN

KINGDOMS OF MERIA BOOK 3

CECELIA MECCA

ALTIORA Press

TAKEN
BY THE
ELDERMAN

A LEGENDS OF MERIA NOVEL

CECELIA
MECCA

To Blood and Brawn, love you all!

AUTHOR'S NOTE

If you've read and enjoyed my books in the past, please join my newsletter to stay up to date with this brand new series. Also receive a map of Meria as a part of the bonuses for this book!

SIGN UP HERE

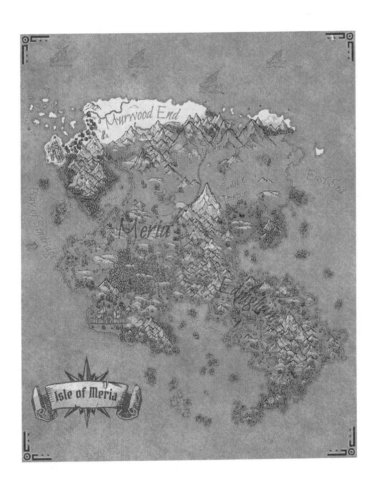

HILLA

Craighcebor, Kingdom of Meria
"Get your hands off of me."

I did not survive these past two years to be taken prisoner now.

My sister's men are mere yards away from us. But as I open my mouth to scream, tis promptly covered by a gloved hand.

I saw my opportunity to escape as my husband cowered inside the blacksmith's shop. He yelled for me to return inside, of course. But I knew there was help to be had. All I needed to do was get to one of my sister's men.

The queen's men.

One glimpse of the glorious Tree of Edingham on one of the men's surcoat, spotted through a crack in the closed window, was all I needed to summon the courage to finally leave the loathsome man responsible for me being here, in the thick of battle.

Ignoring the screams and relentless clanging of swords between my hateful husband's men and innocent Merians that surely spell death for some, I sprinted to the door of the darkened shop, where Whitley hid like the coward he is, and tossed it open—and was at once grabbed from behind.

Now I try to turn around, to see my attacker. But his hands are like wrought-iron vices. One of his arms encircles my waist as he drags me effortlessly away from my salvation.

When I was accused of adultery, I did not fight.

When I was excommunicated from court, I did not fight.

When my husband came to my bed, I did not fight.

But now, as this hooded stranger whose robes mark him as an Elderman, drags me away from my sister's men, away from the only thing I've lived for these past two miserable years—to be reunited with Cettina—I fight like the devil.

"Be still."

His voice is like a whip cracking against my resistance.

Farther and farther from the fight we move until the edge of the small village is just out of running distance. If he manages to get me into those woods, I am lost. And so, with every bit of strength, I push against his arm. To no avail.

Attempting to bite his cupped hand, and failing, I watch as the very husband who made my life hell these past two years is dragged from the blacksmith's shop by the queen's retinue, taking him captive for this unauthorized attack against the Merian village. As always, I do not fear for myself.

Nothing this man could do to me, short of slitting my throat, could compare to all that I've gone through since the day my father announced my betrothal to the aging Lord Whitley of the Edingham Borderlands. But without my account of what happened here today, the bastard could very likely use his silver tongue to escape persecution. Again. Whitley's treachery against my sister must be exposed lest she remain in danger. Cettina must know he ordered the attack to draw Edingham into a war with Meria. One my sister does not want.

I hear the horse before I see him. Panic wells inside my chest, bubbling to the surface. Does he plan to take me with him? Why?

I cannot leave this border town. Not with Cettina's men so close by.

Think, Hilla. Think.

He cannot get me on that horse and keep me silent all at once. We are not so far away from the village that my screams will go unheard. Tis my only chance.

But then, I am let go.

Taking a deep breath after being trapped by my kidnapper, I prepare to run. Until I see the reason for my release.

Two men, my husband's men, are approaching from behind. Swords drawn, they stare down my abductor without a glance at me.

"Give her to us."

Though one is hardly known to me, I am quite familiar with the taller of the two. One of many who's guarded my door every step of our loathsome journey from our home at Redmare Castle to the ill-fated village of Craighcebor, his cruelty matching that of his master's with no care for my well-being.

"She comes with me." That emotionless response, from my captor, makes me curious to see his face. From my vantage point, I see only deep brown robes and a hood. What does the Elderman want with me? I'm not so naive to think his intentions are pure. Under the current Prima's leadership, the actions of many of these supposed "men of God" leave much to be desired.

When my husband's men step forward toward us, the Elderman warns them.

"One step closer and this morning's sunrise will have been your last."

3

My captor's words manage to sound menacing but not exaggerated. As if he means each and every one.

But one churchman against two armed knights?

Tis only when the Elderman draws his sword that they stand down. My husband's men, those with no qualms about attacking a village of innocents, men who appeared a moment ago so mighty and strong, turn and run.

They sprint in the opposite direction, leaving me alone with . . . not a simple Elderman. I'd not noticed his sword. My feet remain still even though this is my opportunity to run. He turns to me, his face still obscured by the hood.

"You are a Shadow Warrior," I say.

His nonanswer is my answer. I resign myself to this new fate, for resistance to such a man would be the height of futility.

2

AIKEN

*T*hat we are feared even more than we are revered worked in my favor today. Though I had two plans to get the lady onto Sorel without attracting attention, her sudden acquiescence made the task much simpler.

But now, as she—the traitorous sister of the queen—sits practically on my lap as we ride, rattling off question after question, none of which I've thus far answered, I wonder if I'd been too hasty when I decided against tying a rag around her mouth.

"Answer me," she demands, as if she were the queen herself.

Since getting as far away from Craighcebor is my only concern, I try to block out her questions and concentrate on those who might be following us, but her constant barrage is beginning to grate.

I've seen the queen only twice, but not in the past several years. Unlike Cettina, a strikingly beautiful woman with blonde hair so light some call it unnatural, Hilla, her hair a darker shade, might seem to pale in comparison. But her full lips are hard to ignore. Her hair, neither blonde nor brown.

Her shape, neither slim nor thick. All the same, I recognized her immediately. Even if she'd not been hiding in that smithy's shop with her equally traitorous husband, I could have identified her as the queen's sister. Clearly raised at court, the daughter of a king, her mannerisms mark her as more than a mere noble.

"Where are we going?" she demands yet again.

Ignoring the question, I slow our mount nearly to a stop. Although not the main road, this particular path is well-traveled enough to cause concern, and I've detected a presence. Moments later, a deer sprints out from the dense woods, directly in front of us, disappearing almost as quickly.

"How did you know he was there?"

After more than an hour, finally a question I am able to answer.

"A change in the sound of the woods."

I spur our mount forward.

"He speaks. Finally."

I do not answer, as there is no need. Speak only when necessary. Answer only when your words cannot be used against you. Two of the many, many lessons I received in training all those years ago.

After a moment passes without me elaborating on those words, Lady Hilla makes a strangled sound of frustration, and I'm brought back to that day when Baldric Orazio began to instruct me.

"If you are to complete your training, you cannot be simply another warrior. A skilled swordsman. Or bowman. This isle has plenty of both. But you must be more than that. Your secret weapon, my son, are these." My mentor pointed to my ears. "You cannot listen if you are speaking."

Minutes turned to hours with none but that single deer as our witness. Lady Hilla, now squirming in front of me, her

6

backside reminding me I'm still very much a man, finally reached her limit.

"Either you answer some of my questions, or I will jump from this horse."

Listening less to her words than the tone of her voice, I conclude the lady is serious. She is actually considering such a thing. And although that would solve the problem of what to do with her, it would leave me with a dead body to attend to.

"You would risk breaking your neck?" I ask, responding with little more than an arch of my brow when she snaps back, "Yes," so quickly. She is speaking from emotion. Not surprising as that is precisely what most people do in situations they cannot control.

"Surely," I say, because tis fact, "you've deduced I do not mean to kill you?"

I'd have told her as much sooner, but then, I've no great desire to reassure a woman who conspired with her husband to incite violence for the sole purpose of starting a war between two kingdoms.

"I would not think a Shadow Warrior, an Elderman, would kidnap a queen's sister either, but alas, here we are."

I'd smile at her sharp wit if I did not think so poorly of the woman.

"Indeed," I say, against my own better judgment. "Here we are."

Knowing I must offer at least some bit of information lest the woman actually carry out her threat, I tell her only what she needs to know.

"I do not plan to kill you. We will stop as soon as I deem it safe."

Though I thought the explanation sufficient, she continues with more questions.

"Why did you take me? What do you plan to do with me? Where are we going?"

It has been an excessively long day. My head began to throb hours ago. And though we've actually started back-tracking toward Craighcebor along a different path, and are indeed traveling toward Edingham—a fact that Lady Hilla does not seem to realize—there is always a possibility Whitley's men could still be looking for her.

Not to mention the queen's.

I'd considered some time ago taking her directly to Queen Cettina's men to let them deal with the traitor. She cannot come with me to the Merian court, of course, so I will need to relinquish her into Cettina's care. But first, once I am sure we are not being followed, I will learn the truth of her actions. Learn precisely how large a threat she is to her sister's rule.

This woman will share any secrets she holds. And as the wife of one of the most hated men on the Isle, Lady Hilla may provide valuable insight into his goal and that of his warmongering allies.

"They say," she begins again, "you are the deadliest of warriors in all of the kingdoms."

Nay, that accolade belongs to another group of men, although the warriors who fight for the church are highly skilled indeed. I wait, curious where she intends this new argument to lead.

"They say the Prima's Shadow Warriors could overwhelm any of King Galfrid's men, and my sis—the queen's as well, at the same time. And quite easily."

She thinks I do not know her identity. This time, I do smile. How very much Lady Hilla has to learn.

"They say none see you coming. That you could raise your sword before the enemy even has a chance to blink."

I say nothing but silently agree with her assessment.

"Why then, would an Elderman, a Shadow Warrior, a man whose skills are superior to all others, waste such talents on a lowly woman such as me?"

Two things become apparent to me with her question.

Lady Hilla believes that flattery will advance her position. A belief that is not all that surprising given that she is married to a man who loves himself above all things. Such a tactic must have worked well with Whitley.

Second, she believes that disparaging herself as a woman might gain my trust. Indeed, there are men who feel themselves superior because of their gender. The man I serve, the leader of the church, is such a man.

Since she cannot see my face, I allow myself to smile. If she knew who I truly served, knew my life's purpose, Lady Hilla would not make such a remark. One I know she does not believe herself.

Tis not because of her questions that I slow once again to a stop. This is as good a place as any to camp for the night. To begin my interrogation.

Lady Hilla has questions, but I do as well. Ones she will answer.

Of that I have no doubt.

3

HILLA

I could run.

He left me by the stream to take care of my "needs." An entire day with the man and still I've not seen his face, shadowed as it was with a cowl. He spoke little, despite my repeated questions, but from his voice it seems the Elderman is not overly old.

Dipping my hand in the cold water, I splash it on my face. Then, cupping my hands, I drink deeply. The Elderman did attempt to give me his waterskin, but I refused it, though I know that depriving myself of water, like tossing myself from his horse, will do little good if I'm to get back to Cettina.

Surely Whitley will have been captured by now. My sister's men were everywhere and appeared to have been prepared for the attack somehow. Though no thanks to me. If so, they will know of my husband's involvement. But what if he is able to convince them of his innocence? I must get back to her, to tell Cettina all that I know. Edingham is no friend to Meria, but neither would the queen ever attack innocent villagers. Nay, Whitley attempted to provoke a war between our kingdoms, and Cettina must be told all that I've learned.

Standing, I look toward the small fire. Even summer nights are not immune to cool temperatures, and as the sun begins to set, the warmth of that fire calls to me. Turning toward it, knowing I'd not make it far alone, without a horse, in woods I do not know, I walk back to the makeshift camp.

The smell of roasted rabbit hits me as I approach.

It seems unlikely I shall be raped, or killed, by this Elderman. No Shadow Warrior would contemplate such a thing, if the stories are to be believed. They are the church's warriors. Highly skilled, thanks to the best training on the Isle. No tales of their cruelty, thankfully, have reached my ears.

On the other hand, he took me against my will. And is a man who could easily overpower me, more so than most. Even so, running now will yield me little.

"How did you know I'd not run away?" I ask, approaching the fire. Still hooded, the Elderman sits with his back to me. Unsurprisingly, he does not answer.

Although I do not wish to be near him, I find myself moving toward the log he's clearly positioned as a makeshift seat for me.

"What kind of man takes a woman against her will," I ask, sitting, "and then fetches a seat for her near the fire?"

No answer. Damn the man.

"Do you ever take that thing down?" I ask, darkness descending quickly, making him appear even more ominous than usual.

I could not be more astonished when he reaches for his hood. Without comment, of course. At times I wonder if he hears me. But clearly he does now, and when the Elderman lowers the cowl, I lean forward, not trusting my own vision.

Firelight flickers across his features, a square jaw set as I'd imagined given his lack of speech. His lips pursed. His eyes,

11

though I cannot discern their color, light and piercing. His hair tied back at the nape of his neck.

Cold. Emotionless.

Exceedingly handsome, and not at all what I'd expect an Elderman to look like. Certainly, he is no elder. Perhaps just a handful of years older than I? He's not seen more than thirty and five summers, if that many.

He turns from me, returning his attention to the rabbit roasting at the end of his stick. Is his efficiency any surprise? While I managed to get a drink and wash my face, the Elderman caught dinner and started a fire.

"Why did you take me?" I try again, not expecting an answer, somehow more unsettled now that his face has been revealed.

"Why were you in Craighcebor this morn?"

"Why were you?" I counter. If ever I wished I were my sister, now is that time. She is the only woman I know with the ability to intimidate a Shadow Warrior. But I am not Cettina.

Tis why she is queen, and I am the wife of a man such as Whitley.

"You snatch me from—"

"Precisely what did I snatch you from? What were you doing cowering in that blacksmith's shop?"

This is a man accustomed to getting answers. I owe him nothing, and yet . . . a prickling of fear that had been mostly absent these past few hours returns.

He is a Shadow Warrior, Hilla. No man on this isle is deadlier than he. Do not let him lull you into believing you are safe.

"The battle," I say as if my answer is so obvious that he should not have had to ask it. I will give him no more than that.

"Why were you there?" He twists the rabbit around, and my mouth begins to water. I've had nothing to eat this day.

I summon the courage that Cettina would surely have if she were sitting on this log. Raising my chin, I tense, prepared to accept the consequences of my words.

"I will answer no more of your questions, Elderman. Not until you tell me why I am here."

He looks at me for so long, my hands begin to shake. I tuck them under the folds of my riding gown to hide them, but he no doubt notices.

The man sees everything.

He pulls the stick back so suddenly, I think for a moment he is coming for me. Instead, he tears meat from the end of it, leans over and hands a piece to me.

I take it.

Eating in silence, I wonder why he's started a fire. My husband's men did not do so on our journey to Craighcebor. But then, they were attempting to avoid notice, slinking through the countryside toward the Merian border. As usual, Whitley kept me close to his side, though he was careful to say nothing in my presence. Only by hiding in the shadows did I learn anything at all.

I watch, and wait. I may not have Cettina's fearless nature, but I did inherit our mother's share of patience. One cannot have all the virtues, she was fond of saying when I would wish to be more like my sister.

"You balance each other, my daughters," she would say.

Staring into the fire, I can see her, an older version of my sister with her long, pale locks always flowing nearly to the small of her back. The day she died, all of Edingham wept, Cettina and I alongside them. She'd kept father in check, somehow. Not, certainly, in any outward way. He ruled as king of Edingham without ever asking for her council. And yes, she gave it, but in such subtle ways Father never guessed her intentions.

When she died, even he mourned. And our kingdoms paid the price for her loss.

Feeling his eyes on me, I look up, suddenly aware the Elderman must have been watching me for some time. He inspects me as one would a berry, determining if it offers sustenance . . . or poison.

"You are Lady Hilla Borea, daughter of the late King Malcom, sister to Queen Cettina of Edingham. And wife to Lord Whitley of the Borderlands."

He knows my identity. "You took me for ransom."

Some say the church has more coin than the kingdoms of Meria and Edingham combined. So it would seem a risky endeavor to risk my sister's anger for more of what he does not need.

Father Silvester and his Elderman move freely throughout the Isle. Enemies since the Kingdom of Meria split into two, Merians and Mountain Men, as those in Edingham are known, very rarely cross the border. While those in Murwood End to the north travel freely to both southern kingdoms, we do not venture into Meria often. Some traders do, of course. But none other, except the church, collecting coin along the way.

"Then you know my sister will be most displeased by your actions?"

I had not wanted to give him leverage by revealing my identity, but if he already knows...

"No, I am helping her. I think she will be grateful to me for keeping her guarded."

He says it with no emotion, no judgment. In fact, it takes me a moment to decipher the words. Is this man actually suggesting . . . ?

"Safe?" I explode, forgetting for a moment to whom I speak. "You think to keep Cettina safe from me?"

The Elderman is back to not answering.

Refusing to look at him, to acknowledge him, I consider his words. I consider all I know of the man he serves, as the Shadow Warriors are the Prima's army.

I've met Father Silvester on many occasions. When my father was alive, the Prima came to court regularly. Although he primarily resides in Avalon, a port town on the west coast in Meria, he and his men traveled to Edingham often. The church owns properties throughout the Isle, all of which benefit from being free from taxation.

While he and Father enjoyed an amicable relationship, the Prima and my sister do not. She feels they have grown too powerful, Father Silvester too invasive. Does he mean to assert his power over my sister by taking me captive? Then again, how could this have been planned? There was no way for the Elderman to know I would be traveling with my husband.

By rights, I should not have been there, in the midst of battle. Only a monster like my husband would put a woman, his wife, in such danger—unarmed, with no way to defend myself, the consequences evident as I sit here this moment.

A captive.

So if it was not planned, what does this Elderman think to gain? And does he truly believe he is aiding my sister, as if I am a threat to her?

My hand drops, the last few bites of meat still gripped in my fingers. "You believe that I was complicit in the attack?"

He watches me but says nothing.

My shoulders sag in relief. We are on the same side, this Elderman and I. He just doesn't know it yet. At the moment, he thinks I approve of my husband's vile actions. And that I would condone an attack on innocent villagers, even if they are Merians, simply to provoke a war. One that Meria started, and which some in Edingham aim to finish.

Some, like my husband, will never forgive the fact that King Galfrid of Meria sent more than two hundred warriors into Galmouth Bay. Indeed, if that ship had not sunk, Galfrid's own son along with it, those men would have unleashed devastation on my people unlike anything we've seen in years.

But the ship never made it.

This, however, does not excuse men like Whitley who hate the fact that my sister has not retaliated.

"You believe I condoned the attack." This matter is so easily cleared. "And you took me to protect the queen."

Why? The Prima has never been interested in helping my sister before. But that is a matter for a different time.

"I love my sister." I lean forward. The Elderman's steady gaze fumbles my words. "I would never, ever do anything to hurt her. My husband's actions are his own."

I smile. By tomorrow, I will be with Cettina once I convince him we are on the same side. Tis a relief to realize as much.

"Surely if you know me, then you know I did not choose him. My father betrothed me to the vile man. And since we left court, I've done nothing but attempt to help my sister, to *feed* her information, at great risk of being discovered. So you see," I finish, "we are on the same side. You can return me to her tomorrow, and Cettina will vouch for all that I say."

For the first time all day, I can breathe easily. Taking a bite of rabbit, I wait for him to respond. To declare that we will, in fact, turn back around. To acknowledge that this has all been a great misunderstanding.

His eyes narrow. This Elderman is, indeed, a good-looking man. The church should have a rule against such a thing. Tis unnatural.

Although he looks quite intimidating, I continue to smile at him. Elated to realize we are not at odds, after all.

"You, my lady, are a liar."

4

AIKEN

a beautiful liar. But a liar nonetheless.

I turn away from her look of shock. She is a good liar, to be sure. Cunning, this sister of the queen's. Of course, what else could I expect from a woman who had an affair, was subsequently excommunicated from court because of it, and then traveled with her husband to lay witness to an abhorrent attack?

Whitley's men would no doubt have killed innocents, just as they did in their first attack at Saitford.

"How dare you?"

I open my eyes to see my lovely captive jump from her seat, feigning indignation. She begins to pace, likely realizing her position. She is trapped.

But right on one account.

Taking her captive, even if done to protect her sister the queen, will do little to quell the tumultuous relationship between Edingham's sovereign and the Prima. I've thought of many ways to explain the situation to Father Silvester and more than one possibility presents itself.

Though none do little to quiet the most pressing of concerns.

What do I do with Lady Hilla?

When I saw her at the smithy, preparing to escape, I did not hesitate. Whitley's accomplice could not get away.

Aye, I could have taken her to the queen's men. But, reluctant to reveal myself, my own mission partly hinging on stopping the attack on Craighcebor, I chose to carry her away from the fray. And now I'm intent on learning precisely how much of a threat she poses.

Overcome with emotion, Lady Hilla continues to pace around the campsite, muttering to herself. Finding myself staring boldly at her, I turn away quickly from the ample bosom I've no right to look upon. From her full lips, which God surely intended to be kissed.

A cunning, beautiful traitor.

How I wish there were time to let myself fall into a deep sleep, to make up for the little I've had these past few days, before attempting to interrogate this woman.

"Sit," I say with the full expectation of being obeyed. My position within the church guarantees it. From the day I was sworn to protect the Prima, and the church, in that order, I've been both feared and respected in equal measure. Each day, as my colleagues kneel in prayer, my fellow soldiers and I train. All day, every day. Unless we are sent out on a mission.

Shadow Warrior.

Tis not a name we use for ourselves, but tis an accurate one nonetheless. We move without being seen. Which means none, with the exception of the Prima himself, truly knows where we are located, or who we serve, at any given time.

A fact Silvester has exploited more and more of late.

Unsurprisingly, the lady sits.

"You claim to love your sister and yet you aid your husband in instigating an attack that will undoubtedly see Edingham at war."

Lady Hilla wants to be brave. She glares at me, wishing to lash out. And yet, she holds back. Her sister would not do so. But then, her sister wields more power than most.

"You claim," she says, gathering her skirts, now muddied at the hems, around her ankles, "to serve the Prima. To be a man of God. And yet you take an unarmed woman captive."

I never claimed either of those things, but I will not point out such a fact to her.

Like most people, silence unnerves Lady Hilla.

"I will answer your questions, Elderman," she spits out, the fire crackling in front of us. I'd not have lighted one had I thought anyone might encounter our camp. But here, so far off the main roads, I am certain we are safe.

For now.

"But you must tell me your name."

An easy enough request to fulfill.

"Father Aiken."

She blinks. As expected, the name means nothing to her.

"Father Aiken," she repeats, her voice low. Sensual, one might say. "Why does the Prima care suddenly for my sister's well-being?"

He doesn't.

She scowls. "Very well. I did not aid my husband. I was as unwilling to be in Craighcebor as I am here, right now with you."

I wait for her to continue.

"He never allows me to leave his sight when we travel," she insists. "Ever."

"Including taking you to battle? You can understand my reluctance to believe such a thing."

"I care little for your beliefs, Elderman."

I lean forward. "Why ask for my name if you do not intend to use it?"

This time, tis Lady Hilla who remains silent.

"Shall I remind you, your fate is in my hands, Lady Hilla."

My words have their intended effect.

"Nay, *Father Aiken*, it is not."

Whether she refers to God, or something different, I know not. But not for the first time today, I find something to respect in a woman I very much dislike.

She could be forgiven for having an affair, given Lord Whitley's repulsive countenance, not to mention his advanced age. And if she truly was taken to that village by force, tis possible the lady is innocent of complicity.

But one thing I cannot forgive. Remaining with such a man. Rumor has it the queen attempted to welcome her sister back to court after their father died. But the lady refused.

Why stay with him if not because his beliefs aligned with her own? Divorce is not unheard of here on the Isle, and certainly not if your sibling is the queen.

"Tis late." Without another word, I ready myself for the eve. Taking off the thick robes that mark me an Elderman, I lay them down on the ground close enough to the fire to gain some warmth but not so close to risk getting burned.

After adding another log to the fire and stoking it, I lie on the ground with nothing under me but my robes. "There is a bedroll laid out already," I say, unable to see her. "Go to sleep."

Trained to listen closely, I can tell when she stands, where she moves, and that instead of moving toward the bedroll, Lady Hilla is above me instead.

I crack my eyes open.

"Aye?"

Hands on her hips and glaring down at me, for the first time today, I see the resemblance. Their hair may be different shades. Their faces, similar, though not the same—Lady Hilla more ample, and in some ways, more appealing. But now, standing above me, they are one and the same, she and the queen.

"You would simply close your eyes and sleep? Giving me no answers. No indication of where we are or where we are going. What you intend to do with me. Nothing more than, 'Go

to sleep'? You are either daft or delusional to think I will simply lie on that bedroll and—"

I jump to my feet so quickly, Lady Hilla nearly falls backward in surprise.

Standing close enough to be indecent, though no less so than on our ride here, I say the words that will make quick work of her protest.

"You will go to sleep. Or find yourself brought back to Craighcebor to stand trial with the magistrate for conspiring to incite an attack on their village."

"My sister," she spits back, apparently less afraid of me than she was earlier, "would never allow it. And why are you holding me still if not so that justice, according to you, can be served?"

"Your sister," I remind her, "is queen of Edingham. She has no authority in Meria, less so in the very place that saw innocents slaughtered by the people you think to call on for support."

Her chest heaves with the weight of that truth.

"Go to sleep."

When she raises a hand to strike me, I capture it, my fingers encircling her wrist easily.

"Remember who you deal with, Lady Hilla."

Snapping out of her rage, the lady's eyes widen. She has surprised herself with her actions, and the terror I see almost makes me regret what I am about to do next.

Almost.

5

AIKEN

Firmus maneo.

Easier to repeat in my head than to practice in truth. As I wake, the words come to me, as they do most mornings. I've trained myself to think these words often, even in sleep.

But as I look down on Lady Hilla, the hands I've bound together pulled tightly to her chest, the thin blanket I placed on her after she slept does not alleviate my desire to tread more gently with the woman.

She is more likely in league with Whitley than she is telling the truth. Those ties kept her safe, I remind myself. The rage and despair I witnessed in her eyes last eve were likely a precursor to her attempt at fleeing. Normally I'd have trusted myself to wake the moment she moved. But these past few days have been trying. Sleep, elusive.

Lady Hilla getting herself killed would not do.

First I must discern the threat she poses, and then I will return the lady to her sister—preferably alive. While the journey to Queen Cettina will cause me some delay, it will afford plenty of time for interrogation.

By the time the sun is about to rise, only one thing remains to do before we leave.

"Lady Hilla."

No response.

I squat down beside her, prepared to remove the ties, but instead I pause to watch the queen's sister sleep. Her chest rises and falls as she breathes evenly. Her features, so much softer now. While awake, Lady Hilla's brows are nearly always furrowed, her eyes narrowed.

With good reason, of course.

Once, just two months before joining the Prima's men, I allowed myself to become injured in battle. Having been hired by a border lord to defend against an Eastman's attack, one of many throughout the years as the two kingdoms fought for control of the only truly contested land at their border, separated in most places by the Terese River, I was struck in the calf from behind.

Unable to stand, I'd been taken by the victor's men. So I can understand the helplessness Hilla feels now.

As if being summoned from sleep by the silent thought, Lady Hilla's eyelids flutter and open. For a brief moment as she looks at me, I have the ridiculous notion to lean down and kiss her. Never have I seen lips that full on a woman before. She wets them, licking first the top and then the bottom, the pink of her tongue visible for the briefest of moments.

"Bastard," she snaps, lifting her arms to me.

I unbind her silently.

"'Twas unnecessary. And quite uncomfortable," she adds.

I disagree on the first. Though I'm sure she speaks truth to the second.

"You may care for your needs by the stream. We will eat on the road."

"You will not—" she begins. But I'm quick to place my

25

hand over her mouth. I've no time to listen to her arguments. She begins to wriggle underneath me.

"Relieve yourself, and do it quickly," I order. "We are being pursued."

She stands tall, listens, and hears nothing.

"Hurry," I yell, "they may be from Craighcebor."

That fact spurs her along. I turn my back as she flees to the nearest thicket. Moments later, when she re-emerges, I do not hesitate. Riding to her, I lift her up in front of me as her foot reaches the stirrup.

Finally, Lady Hilla hears what I did moments earlier. The distant sound of horses, at least ten or more. Riding away from them—and from the Meria-Edingham border, knowing I am at a disadvantage for having two riders on one horse, I navigate us through the thick woods to the main dirt road. If we are being pursued anyway, we can make better time there.

We stop at a fork in the road sometime later.

"Maybe they are gone?" she asks, hopeful.

"They are not."

On the last ridge, I saw clearly ten, perhaps up to twelve or thirteen, riders. I saw no markings to identify them, though I told her they were from Craighcebor to get her moving more quickly. Perhaps the queen's men? If I could be sure of it, I would stop now. My intent had been to not allow the lady to get away. Perhaps ascertain if she was, indeed, a threat to the queen. Not to travel deeper into Meria. But after an entire morning of doing just that, we are now a long way away from the border.

Lady Hilla is a captive I cannot afford to keep.

But without being certain as to who these riders are, and very much outnumbered, we've no choice.

Taking the road west, we continue as quickly as possible given the circumstances. Lady Hilla says nothing, the pace not conducive to conversation. By the time we stop, she is clearly both angry and uncomfortable.

"We will not stop for long," I inform her. "We're still being followed."

I give her a piece of bread, the last of it. Taking it and eating silently, she watches as I lead my mount to the nearby stream. Both man and horse take advantage of the fresh, clear water. My waterskin refilled, I return to Lady Hilla.

"Why do you wear that hood when there is no one here to see it?"

Not the question I'd been expecting.

"'Tis required. Come, we must not tarry."

A hand on my arm stops me as I prepare to mount once again. The touch, so soft, so unlike any touch to which I am accustomed, is most unexpected.

"I would never harm my sister," she says softly. "Everything I have done has been to protect her. I could have been divorced from Whitley after my father died. When Cettina became queen, she offered as much to me the very day she welcomed us back to court."

She drops her hand, telling me information I know already.

"I stayed with Whitley, monster that he is, for the sole purpose of feeding Cettina the plans he and his traitorous friends concocted. The first attack at the border, at Saitford, the one that King Galfrid retaliated against . . . my husband was one of the men behind it."

I know that fact to be true as well.

"And this attack?" I ask, knowing we have little time for talking.

"He kept it more secretive. I knew he'd been planning something, but it was not until the morning we arrived in Craighcebor, when he instructed me to stay in that blacksmith's shop, that I realized what was happening. He spoke openly to his sergeant that morn. When I saw my sister's men, when I realized the attack had been subdued, I'd planned . . ." She looks directly into my eyes. "I'd planned to go to them, to Cettina's men, when you found me."

"Why were you there at all?" I challenge.

"'Tis as I told you. Whitley did not trust me. He took me everywhere he went. He knew well Cettina had the power to separate us as sure as my father had the power to bring us together. To wed us in the first place."

I turn from her, mounting and lifting her up to me.

Saying nothing, we continue to ride. Though I would prefer it otherwise, our best course of action is to reach Rimstead. A large enough town to hide, if needed.

"You do not believe me still?"

Since I have no answer to her question, I say nothing. By her stiff posture, I know the lady is frustrated. Which indeed speaks to her innocence.

"You've only to bring me to Cettina and she will verify the truth of my words."

It is not the first time Lady Hilla has said as much. And since I begin to believe she may be an unwilling participant in the vile act her husband attempted to commit yesterday morn, I continue to remain quiet.

If Lady Hilla *is* innocent, she will indeed be dismayed to learn we head deeper into Meria, away from the border. I'd have brought her to Breywood Castle, to the queen, if not for the fact that we were being pursued.

God, it seems, has other plans for us this day.

Since when do you attribute the will of God to your actions, Aiken?

There are times, though few and far between, I have managed to quite convince myself I am an Elderman in truth. I've been too long working for the Prima.

Too long in this role.

6

HILLA

"*H*urry," he says as we dismount and enter the wooden gates of what appears to be a fairly large town.

"Where are we?" I ask for the second time.

And once again, he does not answer.

"'Tis maddening," I say, knowing he hears me as we blend into the others. Between two wagons, one loaded with hay bales and the other I cannot discern, we weave our way down the muddied street. The hem of my gown beyond repair days ago, I lift it now only out of habit.

Well-maintained cobblestones line some of the smaller pathways and the front of each building, forming walkways of sorts. Although it is not yet dark, lit wall torches on every building give the town a welcoming quality.

I look at my companion. Never before have I met a man like Father Aiken.

He speaks so little, I rarely know what he is thinking. I would call him cruel, having taken me and later binding my hands, making for the most uncomfortable night of sleep, save the ones Whitley came to my bed, but Father Aiken is not a cruel man.

Handsome beyond measure, strong and obviously quite capable. Keenly observant and more stubborn than most, from what I can discern, but certainly not cruel. Which is why I'd decided to appeal to him, rather than fight him, this morn, telling him the truth. Surely it would help my cause?

"This way."

Hurrying to keep up with him, I marvel at how many of the buildings are made of stone. Not just the larger ones, like the manor house at the end of the street we walk down now, but most of them. The butcher's, the dressmaker's shop. Nearly every one, stone.

Tis a wealthier town than most.

"To where?" I whisper as I'm nearly knocked aside by a boy chasing his friend. "Where are we?" I ask for the third time. Most often I am able to wear him down with repeated questions. Unless . . .

I stop.

He eventually realizes I am not beside him and halts his mount, looking over his shoulder. Always looking over his shoulder. But it does not appear we are being followed. I've not seen or heard the riding party behind us all day.

"Where?" I ask, making it clear I will not move without an answer.

His face is mostly hooded again. But now I know what is underneath and can imagine those piercing eyes boring into me.

"Rimstead."

A sudden coldness hits me at my core.

"Nay."

"Come here, my lady."

The narrow street makes it difficult for him to navigate

with his mount, and he frowns. A hooded Shadow Warrior, his menacing sword ever-present and dangling at his side, his eyes hidden, this is the same man that sent hardened warriors scurrying away. I should do his bidding.

But I do not.

Father Aiken will not harm me. Of that I am certain now.

"Lady Hilla."

He drops the reins and stalks toward me.

"There was little choice as we were being followed. I am as unhappy with the current situation as you. We will speak more on it later. But now, we need to move."

Tis as much as he's said to me all day.

For that reason, I follow him as he turns from me, regains the reins and continues to navigate us forward.

Rimstead.

Well within Meria, no longer along the border. The opposite direction of Breywood Castle. My sister's court is now more inaccessible than ever. I could never reach it on my own. Running away from him was utterly futile.

He needs to believe me. I am certain if he does, the Elderman will return me to Cettina. How and why he helps my sister is still a mystery, but one I suppose I must solve if I am to convince him we are on the very same side.

I follow him to a building at the very end of the road, marked as an inn by the sign dangling from its second story, Crow's End. Before I even see Aiken's hand slip inside his robes, he's handing the boy standing just outside the door enough coin to make him straighten his back immediately.

"Bring him to the stable, see him fed and meet me inside for another when you're finished."

The boy bobs his head enthusiastically, taking the reins. Although I do not see the stable from this vantage point, I assume tis nearby.

"Come," he says, glancing back at me. Our eyes meet, his quiet and as intense as ever. Mine longing for answers. He frowns. "We will speak inside."

We step into the inn, and despite the fact that I follow my captor, and that I'm further away from my sister this eve than I was this morn, I pause to smile.

Tis precisely what I'd imagine an inn to be. Wooden tables with barrels for seats. Dark, wall torches and candles lighting the interior as the sky begins to darken outside. Mostly men, but even a few women, eat and drink and laugh.

"You've not been inside an inn before?"

I finally notice the Elderman staring at me.

"Nay," I admit. "I have not."

As is his custom, he does not seem to believe me.

"My father would never have allowed it," I explain, my new strategy to offer him as much information as possible to bring him to my side. "And my husband kept me more ignorant than even my father. Always feared I would flee from him, with good cause."

We move to the side as a group of men brush past us to leave.

"You said he kept you close?"

Always so suspicious. But instead of taking offense, I simply state the truth.

"He did." Then I turn the conversation back to him. "Is it so common where you are from for ladies to frequent such places?"

The shadow that passes across his features is as much a reaction as I've ever seen from him. Something about that question shook him.

Instead of answering, he turns from me. So very typical. And yet, I do not take offense. I am beginning to think it is his way, to be so brisk, even though I do not understand it.

A man who looks to be at least one hundred years of age

shuffles toward Father Aiken. He whispers something to him and points to the corner of the room. When we are seated at the table, one separated from most others and adjacent to a roaring fire in the hearth, I inquire about the exchange.

"You know him?"

Taking down his hood, the Elderman seems to breathe easier for the first time all day. He looks around the hall and then back at me.

"Aye."

It seems I will get nothing more from him. But then he surprises me by leaning forward, his gaze holding mine.

"We are safe," he says confidently. "Nathan will fetch us a hot meal. And our quarters have been arranged for the evening. You will sleep in a bed this night, Lady Hilla."

A welcome turn of events.

"Now tell me of the affair."

He says the words so casually, I do not absorb them at first.

The affair. Does he mean . . . ?

"Father." I sit up straight in the high-backed wooden bench. "Your question is beyond impertinent."

The old man returns with a young serving maid, who plops two mugs and a pitcher onto our table.

"Many thanks," he says, the man looking at me curiously before shuffling away. How very strange.

"If you'd have me believe that you did not conspire with your husband to facilitate an attack on innocent men and women in order to provoke the Merian borderers into a battle, bringing certain war between the kingdoms"—he pours an ale for us both and slides the pewter mug toward me—"I would argue your account of the events that led to you losing the crown to your sister, indeed, pertinent."

No one has ever asked me such a question directly. Most

whisper and stare and snicker, but none have asked for my account before.

Not even the husband I was accused of having cuckolded.

I'm unsure what to say. Certainly, the truth will not do.

"We have all eve," he says, sitting back. "Do go on."

7

AIKEN

*S*he's already thinking of ways not to answer my question.

Some call Queen Cettina the most beautiful woman on the Isle. And indeed, that reputation is earned. Yet, I would venture to say her sister is even more so. Although there is not one feature, beyond those full lips, that I could point to as evidence of such a claim.

Or perhaps there is one.

Her eyes dart from me to the ale as she thinks. Considers my question. I've been trained to watch the eyes in order to learn a person's true intentions. Words mean little. Anyone can speak them. The Prima, for instance, spouts platitudes about God's will. He claims to love all, that his interest lies purely in saving souls.

Yet his eyes, his actions, tell another story. One of greed and a desire for power so great it threatens to undo all of the good that has been done before him. All of the strides that have been made to bring the kingdoms back to where they first began.

Meria was once the only kingdom on this isle, which was

simply called Meria back then. More than a hundred and fifty years ago, a noblewoman, Lady Edina, sought out a Garra, a love healer, to make the king fall in love with her. He did, and King Onry and Queen Edina's twin sons were later born. When the king later chose his younger son as heir, Prince Aidan, the elder twin by mere minutes, fled Meria with his supporters.

Those men made homes in the previously uninhabited Loigh Mountains. Their community grew. Fifty years and many battles later, the Treaty of Loigh was signed, recognizing the Kingdom of Edingham. With Meria to the west, Edingham to the east, along with the smaller contingent of fierce, independent people who inhabit the frigid north, Murwood End, the Isle was split into three kingdoms, or at least, two official ones.

No king, or queen, reigns in the north. Nor likely ever will.

Although peace has always been a tentative one, when the border village of Saitford was attacked, innocent Merians losing their lives, King Galfrid sent more than two hundred of his best knights across the sea toward Edingham's Galmouth Bay in retaliation. None know what the outcome of battle might have been as the ship carrying Galfrid's only son and heir sank. All but one man was lost.

The tentative peace was threatened once again as Lord Whitley, the husband of my companion, and his warmongering allies thought to recreate the attack on Saitford village in order to provoke a counterattack. For such men, war means instability. Which threatens the queen's rule. Men like Whitley, who see a woman ruler as unnatural, would like nothing better than for Cettina to fail.

Meanwhile, the man I serve, the leader of the church, is a bigger threat than anyone in Meria, or Edingham, realizes. Tis my mission to stop him from seizing more power before it becomes impossible to waylay him. Lady Hilla is not part of my plans.

"You wish for me to believe you're no threat to your sister. And yet, I find you sneaking away from where you were holed up with your traitorous husband. Now, I ask a simple question, and you cannot answer truthfully."

"Simple?" Her nostrils flare. "'Tis anything but a simple question, Father."

I wince internally. I'm long past feeling guilt for posing as an Elderman.

"Aiken. You may call me by my given name."

The lady blinks. "'Twould be disrespectful to do so."

I point out the irony of her words. "Disrespectful to a man who took you against your will?"

She considers that point.

"Very well, Aiken."

I nearly smile at the vitriol with which she says my name.

"You do realize, speaking of my captivity, I could simply begin to scream and alert the others to my identity rather than sit amicably with a man who, as you say, took me against my will?"

I realize the fact well. Which is why I've watched closely for signs of Lady Hilla doing just that.

"Aye, you could do so. But then, you may end up in the hands of a man with ill intentions toward you. One offering his body instead of a hot meal and bed."

Her eyes widen.

"I should be grateful that you've not raped me?"

Although we are separated from most others, the hall is filled with both villagers and travelers. Most ignore us, though a curious few have looked our way from time to time. Mostly wondering, I am sure, what a woman such as Lady Hilla is doing with an Elderman, alone.

"You should consider your options carefully."

She takes a long sip of ale.

"Besides, if you can answer my questions, I will happily give you what you want."

Hilla looks at me, hopeful.

"To return me to Cettina?" she whispers.

Though she may be lying to me even now, her fervent wish to return to her sister plays into the lady's innocence. Either she was an unwilling participant in her husband's duplicities, as she claims, or else Lady Hilla has the utmost confidence that she can convince the queen of her innocence.

Cettina is an intelligent woman. Surely she knows her sister better than any other and can discern any malicious intent.

Of course, those who love us most also have the ability to do us the greatest harm.

"Perhaps if you told me why you are so keen to help my sister I would feel more compelled to answer your question."

I drink slowly, considering my answer. A group of men in the opposite corner of the hall begin to sing. A merry tune, reminding me of a night so many years ago, in a hall very much like this one.

I knew so little then.

"What were you doing there? At that attack?" she asks.

I refill my mug, surprised to see hers empty as well. As I'm about to answer, the serving maid brings us two meat pies. The welcome respite could not have come at a better time. I can give her no real answers, and so, I give her something else instead in between bites.

Something to earn her trust.

"I am the son of a prostitute. Raised in a whorehouse in Galona. I've no notion who my father might be, nor does it concern me. Once, at ten and two, I was beaten so badly by an older boy for a loaf of bread I refused to give up that my mother was certain I would not live. She and her friends tended to me, saved me."

She watches me, eating in silence.

"You asked if it is common where I'm from for ladies to frequent places such as this. Aye, Lady Hilla, the women I knew would think nothing of frequenting the Crow's End. Or other places considered much more scandalous than this well-tended inn and tavern."

I've told that story to no one but the man who took me away from Galona. Who saved me. Who I serve this day, and all my days.

As a reward, Lady Hilla speaks her own truth. I can see the evidence of it in her eyes.

"I did not commit adultery against my husband," she starts. "Despite his advanced age and—" She looks down, her cheeks reddening. "That is to say . . ." She looks up once again.

"I was raised in a whorehouse, Lady Hilla. Nothing you could say will shock me, I assure you."

"But . . ." Her full lips purse together. "You are an Elderman."

Damn, but I am not. And am reminded of that fact just now as she looks at me.

"I understand what you are attempting to say. Go on."

She nods quickly, grateful.

"And you know already, he is not a nice man."

I make a very ungentlemanly sound at that. Lord Whitley is the very epitome of evil. Her description of him, generous.

"But still, I was not unfaithful to him."

She speaks the truth.

Breaking our eye contact, she takes another bite and I do the same. We finish eating, the song long ended, with others having taken their place. Here, in this town, in this hall, the border battles and court politics seem so far away.

And yet, they are not. Everyone here is in danger if Father Silvester and men like Whitley, those who would consider personal gain over the good of the Isle, have their way.

"Your father had an innocent man beheaded, then?"

On this, she hesitates.

"There is more to the story?" I ask.

We're interrupted as our meals are taken away. In the flurry of activity, I look to the innkeeper, who shakes his head. If we were being followed, our pursuers have not come into town. The gates are closed at sundown, and though the sky has not yet completely darkened, tonight they close early.

For us.

For me.

"Aye," she admits, "there is."

Sighing, she sits back against her seat, seemingly unaware that her life might have been in danger this day. If the men that followed us were truly from Craighcebor, they'd care not that Lady Hilla is the queen's sister. Or that Cettina's men prevented the attack on their village. Sometimes facts can be misplaced until it is too late. I've seen more than one innocent be tried, and executed, too quickly.

I watch her as she lifts the mug to her lips. Her eyes catch mine and quickly look away.

"We will stay here until I can be sure you are not followed. One or two days, at most."

When the lady begins to protest, I cut her off.

"And then I will escort you to Breywood Castle."

Her hand stills as she places the pewter mug back onto the table between us.

"You will?"

The delay will be difficult to explain. But I'd not trust anyone else with her escort.

"I will."

"You believe me?"

"I am as certain as I can be without proof that you did not aid your husband in his most recent endeavor."

Her tears surprise me. The lady has fought me, berated me, and despite knowing who and what I am, has provoked me still. Aye, she had been scared at first. And angry that I bound her hands. But she has stayed strong despite it.

I could withstand a battle-axe being swung at my head. A sword pointed at my heart. But tears. Nay, not them.

Wiping them away, she breathes in deeply and swallows to regain her composure. She does so quickly, reminding me this is no ordinary woman. I sit across from the eldest daughter of King Malcom of Edingham.

She'd been raised to become a queen.

"Father," the serving maid interrupts once more. "I am to tell you the bath you ordered has been drawn. I am happy to escort the lady to your chamber."

Hilla's eyes fly to mine.

She asks the silent question, and I do not answer with words. Although I do not believe she will flee, tis still safest if she remains with me. Weighing the decision against the appearance of impropriety, there is no other choice.

The queen's sister, duplicitous or nay, will not be harmed on my watch.

She does not move.

"As you've ordered it, I might very much enjoy a hot bath," I say.

She shoots up so quickly, I cannot help but smile. Without further prompting, Lady Hilla follows the maid. Although my back faces most of the hall, I pull my hood up anyway, out of habit.

My brothers would do well to adopt this particular custom, the hood an easy way to remain hidden. None seem to look my way, thankfully. We will need to remain inconspicuous while we are here—too long a time, given my mission. I need to be away from here, seeking out news of the Merian court. Of the king's nephew and Silvester's whereabouts. This delay may prove a costly one, but there's no hope for it. If we leave too soon, tis likely the men following us will be lying in wait.

Two days.

In two days I will leave to return her to court, as she does not appear to be a threat to her sister. In the meantime, I share a bedchamber with Lady Hilla. Who is likely at this very moment disrobing for her bath.

I pour myself another ale.

8

HILLA

*S*tepping from the tub, I take the drying cloth the serving maid left behind. Capable and efficient, she'd make a fine lady's maid. For an inn such as this, in a small town with nothing near, save the border more than two days' ride to our east, my needs have been more than met.

The meal, delicious. The bathwater, hot. The maid Coraline even left behind a bar of lemon-scented soap. Or perhaps, being my first time in such a place, I am simply as unworldly as my husband accused me of being.

This may be my first inn, but I am hardly sheltered. When Mother was alive we traveled the Isle. To Murwood End, even. To the Tournament of the Loigh. To the Highlands of Edingham. But when Whitley's daily insult of "harlot" failed to rile me, he tried many, many others.

Having lost his fortunes and then regained them, marriage to the king's daughter was to have been his greatest achievement. And it was, for a time, when my father named Lord Whitley an honorary member of his Curia. Even though he had no official role in Father's council, his ability to attend meetings of the Curia was an honor indeed.

And then, the affair.

Pushing such thoughts from my mind, I move to the bed. Not expecting to find my gown as the maid kindly offered to have it laundered, I had planned to don my shift but it too is missing. Partly grateful because she must be laundering it as well, I have little time to debate alternative clothing to wear before a knock at the door has me scurrying around the chamber.

Tis nowhere. She took all of it. My gown, my shift and stockings. The only thing remaining are my boots, which do me little good now.

"Lady Hilla?"

Tis Aiken, as expected.

I could hide under the bedcovers, but then how would he enter? The maid instructed me to lock the door behind her, a wise directive.

"Do you have a key?" I shout through the thick wooden door.

"Why should I need a key if you can simply open the door?" he asks.

I look frantically toward the bed.

"Do you have a key?" I ask again.

"Lady Hilla, open the door."

More accustomed to his brisk manner, I ignore his gently tone and flee to the bed. Tossing the drying cloth to the bottom of it, I climb inside. The bed is surprisingly soft, the feather mattress rivaling my own at Redmare Castle. My dreadful home these past few years.

Realizing he must have a key, praying he does, I am not surprised to see him angered once the door finally does open.

"What game do you play at?" he asks, stalking inside.

Finding me with the firelight and candles as his guide, Aiken walks toward the bed.

"Are you—"

"The maid took my clothing. All of it. I'd assumed she left my shift, but . . ." I lift the covers up to my chin. To think about it. A married woman alone, nude, with an Elderman. Unfortunately, this could not even be considered the most scandalous moment of my life.

My hair is still wet, though I dried it as much as I was able, and tis soaking the pillow beneath me, but I don't dare reach up to pull my hair up over my head. I'd had no time to dry it properly, and probably should not have washed it. But every bit of me dearly needed scrubbing.

Looking away, he stalks back to the door.

"I will fetch your clothing."

"Please, no."

Aiken spins back around.

"I will not move from under the coverlet. Please. I am unused to being so dirty, and she's laundering my clothing."

Aiken pulls back his hood, revealing that perfectly shaped jaw always so set and serious.

"You cannot remain as such until morning. I will remain in this chamber, for your protection."

I already knew as much.

"I can." Turning in the bed, I close my eyes. "You may bathe while tis still warm. I will keep my eyes shut."

Although I cannot see him, I hear nothing and know Aiken remains still.

"Please do not tell me you worry about decorum? I cannot be more ruined than I am already."

Still, no movement.

"Aye," he says softly. "You can."

I think back to what he told me belowstairs. Of his upbringing. And immediately regret my words. Even misused as I've been, my husband attempting to beget a child when the mood struck him, he'd never been violent with me.

Threatened it many times, but not once did he strike me. At least, not with his hand. The many lashes against my soul are another matter entirely.

"I shouldn't have said that. I spoke out of turn. I know there is worse. I know you've seen worse."

He makes a dismissive sound. Presumably he has begun to undress. I hear his soft movements, but as always, Aiken is as stealthy as any man I've ever met.

"Was it . . . was it terrible?" I venture, tensing.

"My childhood?"

I nod and then realize he does not see me. "Aye."

The clink of boots against the floorboards confirms my suspicions.

"My mother loved me. 'Twas all that mattered."

"How do you mean?"

A splash of water reaches my ears. The very idea of it. Aiken. Nude. And worse, me thinking in such a way about a man that took me captive, a man of God no less.

Perhaps I am a harlot as my husband accused me of being. I may not have had an affair with Lord Bowes, but the thoughts running through my head now are anything but pure.

"You may look," he says. "I am fully submerged."

Indeed, as I open my eyes and shift them toward the tub, I see nothing but his torso. And arms. And shoulders.

Could a man look more different than my husband?

At sixty and seven, Whitley was fit for his age though pale and saggy. But not the Elderman. As he splashes water onto his face, the muscles in his shoulders constrict, the sinew bulging out, emphasizing his incredible strength, his dominance. What power he wields, this Elderman. This Shadow Warrior.

Tis no wonder I'm reminded of the two knights who ran from him. I've no doubt that, had those men in Craighcebor stayed to engage him, Aiken would have easily cut them both down.

Finally, I remember to blink.

"I knew plenty of boys, and girls too, who had not the love of any parent. My mother and the other women cared for me. Fed me. Clothed me and saw me bathed so often I was teased mercilessly by the other children for it. I was not one of them, though. I was . . ." He pauses. "I was no one."

"I am not sure I understand."

He looks toward the stool next to the tub and reaches for the soap. As he does, more of his chest is exposed, and I'm finding it difficult to look away.

"The women were careful not to beget children, and when they did, their babies were taken away. But my mother fought to keep me, her master agreeing because none of the women were more requested than my mother."

He smiles and the effect sends shivers from my wet head all the way down to my toes. What a sight indeed.

"My mother is quite beautiful."

As are you. Although I keep that thought to myself.

"She is alive still, then?"

He seems surprised by the question.

"Aye, very much so."

As he washes, I look away. Not that I want to look away, but tis proper. I focus instead on the fire to his right, again thankful for such a capable maid.

"I am sorry."

The words, so softly spoken, are so different than any he's ever said. I turn back to him. Without his robes, his sword, his face shadowed and menacing, Aiken looks like just a man. Well, perhaps not any man.

I am sorry.

He speaks of my mother.

Unlike the Elderman's past, mine is known to all. He most assuredly knows my mother grew ill one winter and never recovered. The beacon of light for my sister and me in an increasingly dark court fraught with danger from power-hungry men, our mother showed Cettina and me how to ignore it all. How to care for others. To lead without raising the hackles of men who viewed women like my mother, and Cettina and me, very much like the Garra, healers whose gifts grant them a degree of clout denied to most women.

Indeed, the healer's name has become so synonymous with women who wield any sort of power that a new word, something harsher, crueler, came into being, a word I first heard as a child, for any woman with power.

Folgere.

'Twas meant as an insult. A woman who believes in the same tenets as the Garra. Strength. Choice. Love. That a woman embodies all three.

"My mother did not believe as you do," I say, unsure if I should truly say this aloud but already committed. "Like the Garra, my mother scorned the church's belief that women are polluted by their desire for sex and are drawn to men as a result of this pollution."

His hands had been making their way through his wet hair, now loose and reaching his shoulders. Aiken must have removed the tie that held it back when I'd been looking away. They pause now atop his head.

He stares back at me unabashedly. "I do not believe that."

I sit up, now intent in our discussion. With the coverlet still pulled up to my chin, of course.

"Your Prima does. Your church does," I challenge.

"They did not always."

His hands lower into the water with a small splash. "Consider, Lady Hilla, that I was raised by women who earned coin from the use of their own bodies."

"Then what do *you* believe? And tis Hilla, if it pleases you."

He hardly moves in that tub of his.

"Hilla," he tries out, my given name without the title. "I believe a woman, not unlike a man, is free to enjoy or wield or give their bodies as they see fit. As long as that desire does not harm another."

I clutch the coverlet against my neck.

"Then you are at odds with your church."

"Nay," he says. "My beliefs are at odds with the Prima."

Because he is God's representative on the Isle, none, especially not an Elderman, speak out against the head of the church. Some wish to do so, our own Elderman at Breywood among them. But a Shadow Warrior who lives to protect the very man he speaks of? Tis simply not done.

"Should the Prima's man speak out against him?"

"Nay."

"And yet, you do so."

As if realizing he's said more words than he intended, certainly more than I am accustomed to from him, Aiken grinds his teeth, his jaw tensed.

I will get no more from him this eve.

"Close your eyes," he commands.

I do so immediately. A splash tells me he rises from the tub. And since I know the drying cloth is at the foot of my bed, I know, rather than hear, he comes toward me.

The urge to open my eyes is so overwhelming, I nearly give into the temptation. Instead, I wait for him to give me leave to do so.

Moments pass. Convinced he must be clothed by now, I venture the tiniest of peeks. And spy much more than I'd bargained for by giving in to the desire.

His back to me, Aiken is gloriously nude, his backside so

perfectly formed I shut my eyes as tightly as I'm able. So much so it actually hurts to squeeze them tight.

He is an Elderman. My captor.

And I, a married woman.

Truly if I'd not been destined for hell before, I will be after this night.

9

AIKEN

"Took you long enough, *Father*," Nathan quips.

I find the innkeeper in the stables. Though the sun has not yet risen—my companion still slumbering like most of the other inhabitants of the inn—a few have already begun their day.

Including Nathan.

"You've aged a hundred years," I tell him, grabbing the basket of grain. "Have you no stablehands for this?"

Wiping his hands on the front of his tunic, Nathan gladly leaves the task of feeding the horses to me. I greet my own mare first with a pat on the flank.

"We are alone?"

Nathan sits on a wooden stool, apparently content to watch me work.

"Aye, lad."

I've not been a lad for a long time, but to Nathan, his weathered cheeks and long grey beard making him appear as old as the Isle itself, I suppose I am that.

"Care to explain why you travel with the queen's sister?"

I tell the man everything. From attending the Tournament of Loigh at the behest of the Prima, meeting with trai-tors to Edingham on his behalf, to the raid that I myself prevented by warning the queen's guard it was to occur.

Which led to the capture of the queen's sister. The one who claims innocence and yet whose gaze is anything but, especially considering I am, to her at least, an Elderman. But then, if I were to judge her on that merit alone, I am equally as guilty.

Hilla is a married woman. And yet . . .

"There's been no sign of the men who followed you," he says as I move from stall to stall.

"You sent scouts?"

He looks at me as if I am daft.

"We will stay a bit to be sure."

Nathan nods. "Three days?"

"Two, at most. By the time I return the lady to Breywood and make my way east, Silvester will become suspicious of my delay."

Nathan doesn't seem to be troubled. "Tell him you were injured." He smiles, and I see more teeth are missing now than the last I saw him. "I will gladly do the deed myself."

And he could.

To the world, Nathan is an old, kindly gentleman, the innkeeper of the Crow's End. Most would laugh at the prospect of such a man being able to harm one of the Prima's personal guardsmen, a so-called Shadow Warrior.

But I know the truth.

"Thank you for the offer."

I toss the bucket of grain next to him and pull up a stool.

"But I think I will decline."

His smile fades as he waits for me to finish.

I look around the empty stables.

"There is no one," he assures me.

"Although I do not believe she is complicit in her husband's plans, Lady Hilla is hiding something."

"As are we all."

I forge ahead. "Whitley may have been stopped, but there were others in that dovecote to take up his cause."

"The queen must remain steadfast," he says, as if willing it so will make such a thing happen.

"With Stokerton now married to Moray's daughter, their alliance has been renewed, and will help keep the Highlanders in line, I believe. But the Borderers . . ." I've nothing left to say on the matter. The borders are unstable, as they've been in recent years.

"We've more pressing matters than the borders." Nathan leans forward, resting his elbows on both bony knees. "Hinton grows bolder. His supporters can no longer be relegated to the fringes. If Silvester gives him his full support . . ."

Since King Galfrid's son died, his nephew has made no secret of his desire to be named as heir. None, including myself, wish to see such a thing happen. Like the Prima, Lord Hinton cares for one thing alone.

His own interests.

"Then we shall do all we can to see Lord Calderone named as heir."

Nathan makes a sound of disgust.

"He is not a leader of men."

Although I agree, between the two men, there can be no question which is preferable. Which man will serve Meria, and therefore the Isle, better.

"Where does the king stand on the matter?"

Nathan shakes his head. "None can discern, precisely. But these things take time."

We have men, and women, positioned throughout the Isle, but that does not mean communication is easy. The opposite is true, in fact.

"Well," I say, knowing I should return to Hilla before she wakes. "Craighcebor did not, at least, become another Saitford."

Nathan leans forward and slaps me on the back.

"Well done, lad."

"Lord Whitley," I remind him, "is far from being the head of the snake."

Nathan takes a deep, rattling breath in and then pushes against his knees, standing.

"Nay, he is not," he agrees. "You'd best get back to your charge."

"Aye," I say, wondering if I should inquire about her laundered clothing or return without them. *Father* Aiken would indeed fetch her gown and undergarments.

But alas, though I took the vows, I am in reality as much an Elderman as Nathan is just a simple innkeeper. With that thought, I leave the stables and return directly to my temporary lodgings for the next few days.

10

HILLA

I've always awoken before the others, often well before sunrise, while it is still dark enough to need candlelight. Even at Redmare, where my role had been reduced to little more than a minor member of the household. And yet, as I open my eyes, sunlight streams between the wooden slats of the shutters.

I suppose after a sennight traveling with my husband to Craighcebor, then being taken by the Elderman and spending an uncomfortable night sleeping on the hard ground, hands bound, waking late is to be expected.

Realizing I am alone, that Aiken is nowhere to be found, I sit up and immediately spy my clothing lying across the trunk at the foot of the bed. Hastening to dress before he returns, thankful for the clean clothing, I don the undergarments, pulling up each stocking while watching the door.

I've no doubt about how it came to be here.

Aiken has truly earned the moniker by which his kind are known. A shadow, silent and no doubt deadly when necessary. With everything but the ties at my back finished, I move to the bed, intent on straightening the coverlet when the door opens.

"You're not wearing your robes."

He steps inside looking more like one of my sister's commanders than an Elderman.

"If we are being followed, they look for an Elderman and a lady."

When he closes the door behind him, an awareness flushes my cheeks. How many times had I woken last eve aware he slept just a short distance from me? I thought it might have been difficult to fall asleep with that knowledge, but the last thing I remember was him lying on the bedroll he'd placed on the floor.

"You've been out already?"

"Aye. There is no sign of our pursuers. But I believe we should wait until at least tomorrow to ride out. I am only one man . . ."

He does not finish the thought.

"And you do not wish for me to come to harm?" I laugh bitterly.

Aiken moves toward me.

"Even if you were my prisoner still, aye, I'd not wish for you to come to harm."

"Am I not still? Your prisoner?"

He watches as I tie the errant strands of my hair behind me, at the nape of my neck. There's no hope for anything else to do with it now.

"Nay, you are not."

This is news to me. "Nay?"

"I do not believe you were in league with your husband."

I raise my chin. "Good, as I was not."

"I know."

"How?" I demand. "You'd been convinced of it just yesterday."

He looks at me curiously.

"Do you wish to convince me now of the opposite?"

I open my mouth and snap it shut again. Turning, I give Aiken my back.

"I've not seen the maid this morn. She left the clothing but"—I peek over my shoulder—"I cannot tie these myself."

He looks as if he will refuse at first. But then, ever so slowly, Aiken advances toward me. He smells clean. And though he used the same soap as I, anything but womanly. In fact, as his fingers touch the first tie, I close my eyes as if the assault on my senses might not threaten to consume me. But, of course, this does not work.

I can still feel him so close. Slowly he makes his way from the small of my back upward. More quickly than a maid, he claims himself to be finished just moments later. As I spin around, we find ourselves so close I can feel his breath on mine.

Jumping back, though not after picturing what it might be like to kiss a man such as he, I ask how he managed to get done so quickly.

"You forget my upbringing, Hilla."

Of course.

"You've tied many women's gowns."

He neither smiles nor frowns.

"Aye."

"Did they . . . that is to say . . . were you . . ." I stop. Tis not a question for me to ask.

"Was my first time with a woman in a whorehouse?"

My jaw drops.

"You are unlike any Elderman I've ever met, to say such a thing."

Breaking eye contact, he walks toward his belongings and reaches into the leather satchel, muttering something that sounds like, "If only you knew."

I should forget the question. 'Twas as inappropriate as his answer. But instead, I forge ahead, curious. "Aye. I suppose that's what I asked."

There is no *suppose* about the matter. Now that the words are out, I cannot take them back.

Aiken shoves whatever he pulled from his bag into a pocket and crosses toward the door.

"Come, break your fast," he says.

Tis just as well he does not answer. Dressed, refreshed, and no longer a prisoner, I gladly follow. One more day in this town, and we will return to Breywood. My testimony will ensure Whitley is punished for his actions, and he will no longer plot against my sister. I will be married to a traitor to the crown, aye. But no longer will I be his unwilling servant.

"You are in good spirits," he says as I cross the threshold and step into the dim hallway. Aiken locks the door behind me.

"I am pleased you believe me."

"I told you as much last eve."

We walk toward the stairs that lead to the hall.

"But now I know it for certain. And tomorrow, we shall depart for Breywood, and I will soon be reunited with Cettina."

He watches me closely and then holds out a hand, indicating for me to lead us down the stairs. But just as my foot reaches the first step, wood creaking below me, his words stop me.

"I lost my innocence, there, aye. I can tell you the tale belowstairs, if you like."

Laughing, I shake my head at his words. For a man who hardly spoke, tis strange to hear a jest from his lips, as that surely was. But when I look up at Aiken, he is neither laughing, nor even smiling.

"Who are you, Father Aiken? The silent warrior I have known or this other man so very unlike the one who looked at me just yesterday with such suspicion?"

Tis barely perceptible, but the corners of his mouth do lift, if just a bit.

"Perhaps, my lady, I am neither."

11

HILLA

*H*ow very typical.

While Aiken jaunts about town, I am stuck inside this inn. After breaking our fast, he left me in the care of the innkeeper, who kindly gave me a tour of the grounds, and I was able to find the maid who laundered my gown so quickly and thank her. If he thought it odd I remain inside while my companion ventured out, surely he recognized tis not so odd as keeping company with an Elderman.

Aiken explained during the meal that many tavern inns, like this one, pass few judgments over their inhabitants. Like churches, inns tend to be where deals are made. Where gossip spreads. Where people gather, talk and plan.

An air of secrecy permeates this place, a fact which the innkeeper, Nathan, seemed to find amusing when I made mention of it. And now, with nothing to do but to sit and stare out to the street below, I find myself in a similar position to these past few years.

Not that I wanted to attract my husband's attentions any more than necessary. But I'd not been trained to live idly. When it became apparent my mother would have no more children, my father reluctantly accepted that I was to become the first queen of Edingham.

Yet here I sit, captive in all but name only in a remote town further into Meria than I've ever been, save for one visit to the Merian court when I was but a girl. Unable to remain still for much longer, I do precisely what Aiken advised against.

Taking the key he gave me and slipping it into my gown, I make my way down to the hall. Tis midafternoon, and fairly empty still. I spot the innkeeper, who watches me from the corner of the room where he sits with another man about the same age.

Master Nathan waves me over.

I make my way to the innkeeper. Aiken was fairly clear in his instructions that I should speak to no one. And yet, I am not his prisoner. Not any longer.

"Sit with us," he says.

I do so, reluctantly. The barrel is not as comfortable as a cushioned chair, but it will do.

"Lady Julie, may I introduce you to Sir James Stroker?"

Lady Julie.

Aiken must have told Master Nathan to conceal my identity. "I am pleased to make your acquaintance, Sir James."

"The pleasure is mine, my lady," he says, the man's speech more proper than I'd expect from his appearance. "I will admit to some surprise at meeting a noblewoman such as yourself in Crow's End."

Before I can respond, the innkeeper does so for me.

"Sir James was regaling me with news from the border."

Realizing the innkeeper knows more of my circumstances than I'd have imagined, I watch Sir James with interest as Nathan calls a serving maid to us.

"A mug for the lady," he says, turning his attention then to Sir James, as do I.

"I'd not sully the lady's ears with such gossip," he says as the maid returns with a mug. Filling it with the ale from the tankard on the table in front of us, he dismisses Sir James.

"Lady Julie is an adventurous sort. She'd not take offense, would you, my lady?"

"Nay," I assure him. "Do continue."

Though skeptical, the aging Sir James does so.

"I've come from the border, where some say the queen's own brother-in-law has been arrested in Craighcebor."

Pretending to be shocked, I become intensely interested in sipping ale. My mug, a shield.

"Others claim there was a skirmish there, but none seem to know what truly occurred. Something, to be sure."

"To be sure," the innkeeper agrees. "Word will reach us soon enough."

"I suppose it will." Sir James looks at me, and for the first time since arriving, I begin to understand Aiken's caution. In Edingham, I am Queen Cettina's sister. Those who know me would never question my devotion to my sister, even as they may question my morals. But we are not in Edingham. Here, I am an outlaw.

A woman married to the monster who attempted an attack on the very people I now walk among.

Realizing I'd have done better to remain in my room, I stay mostly quiet as the two men talk of raids and alliances.

And ale.

Apparently Master Nathan is also the town brewer as well, not so surprising for a tavern owner.

Nearing the end of my second mug, and more relaxed than I'd been when first sitting down with the men, I'm surprised to feel a presence at my back at the same time that Master Nathan looks over my shoulder.

Knowing precisely who stands behind me, I turn. And look up.

Carrying a leather satchel, still sans robes, Aiken glares down at me. I return his gaze, refusing to be intimidated. I've done too much of that as the wife of Lord Whitley.

"Pardon me," he says with the steely tone I know all too well by now. "My lady. I am surprised to see you here."

As I spin in my seat and catch Master Nathan's expression, though fleeting, it occurs to me that his and Aiken's relationship might be more than simply innkeeper and patron. They know each other. I am suddenly convinced of it.

"We will take the same table as last eve," Aiken says, ignoring me completely now. "Have you taken dinner yet, my lady?"

Though early for such a meal, tis not unusually so. Most take their main meal of the day well before the sun sets, and it seems we will not be an exception. I've eaten nothing since this morn.

"Nay."

The word is hardly out of my mouth before he says, "I will return shortly," and walks away.

Sir James looks between us. Does he think Aiken is my husband? Without his robes, he could easily pass for a knight, or perhaps a commander by his bearing. Certainly no tradesman, his sword marking him a warrior of some sort.

The innkeeper rises, as do I with him.

"Come, I'll see you to your table, my lady."

I am about to tell him I know the way when he leans in close. "Say no more than is necessary."

Did he sense I'd been struggling with how to explain Aiken's presence?

"You are acquainted with him," I whisper back as he escorts me to the same corner table as last eve.

"Aye, Princess," he whispers back.

I sit, staring wide-eyed.

"He told you?"

"He did not have to." The old man winks at me and leaves me to my questions. No other has recognized me. Unlike my sister, I've not traveled widely in many years. I'm accompanied by no retinue and wear no markings on my clothing. Then how?

The same maid who brought me a mug earlier does so again, along with a tankard and second mug. She smiles and walks away as more and more patrons begin to stream inside.

By the time Aiken returns, I've so many questions.

But I start with the most pressing of them all. One that has been on my mind since Sir James told us what he knew of the recent events at Craighcebor.

"Are we in danger?"

When he sits across from me, with his loose linen shirt wide open at the chest, Aiken immediately pours himself an ale.

"Aye, my lady. I believe we are."

12

HILLA

"*I*'ve not drunk so much in one sitting in my life," I confess.

Maybe it was his admission that, aye, we—or more precisely, I—am in danger. That his initial assessment of my involvement in the attempted attack on Craighcebor was not isolated. Apparently he'd spent the afternoon speaking to villagers and his scouts.

Of course my first thought was, why does an Elderman have scouts? But he did not give me any time to dwell on this revelation before launching into what he discovered.

He learned two things.

First, word had already begun to spread that Whitley had been apprehended after attempting to attack the border town and that his wife had gone missing. Apparently, my sister's men still lingered along the border looking for me even now.

Second, the men following us appeared to be following us still, and Aiken did not believe they were my sister's men. They'd not reached this town—yet. He had hoped they would have retreated by now, but apparently that did not happen.

I asked how he learned all of this, and of course, he gave me no answers other than to admit he had help in gathering the information.

Oddly, I remain rather unperturbed by the news. Maybe tis the knowledge that, for the first time in as many years, I am free of Whitley. Having been concerned with my own safety, understandably so given the fact that I'd been taken captive, I'd not thought much beyond my present situation.

But now, knowing Aiken truly does believe me and that he does not pose a danger to me, along with hearing confirmation of the fact that Whitley was apparently still my sister's prisoner, a sense of freedom I've not felt, well, ever washes over me.

Free of Whitley, I can feel the relief blooming within me, but so too a sense of unease, arising from the looming sense of danger. It is a strange mix of emotions. But with every ale I am able to forget both.

"Another, my lady?" the serving maid asks as she takes away our empty tankard.

I look at Aiken, who says nothing.

"Aye, if it pleases you, Mistress Coraline."

When she smiles at my use of her name, her teeth not completely straight, tis a beautiful sight. I've not met a person before who isn't more pleasing to look at when they smile.

Except Whitley, of course. When my husband smiled, 'twas usually cause for concern.

The inn fills, the workday now done. My eyes wander to a man standing near the door as if on guard.

Aiken's words draw my attention back. "You remembered her name."

There was a man once, perhaps five or six years ago, who came to court from Murwood End. He was large, like Aiken.

And extremely handsome. He looked at me all through the meal, and my insides felt then as they do now.

At the time I thought the Voyager was the most handsome man on the Isle. Even more so than Cettina's commander, whom all the women at court swooned over. But even he did not hold the appeal that this Elderman does for me.

Such a silly thing, to stare at a man who'd pledged his troth as thoroughly as I had to Whitley. Aiken was married to God, and I've no right to stare at his chest so.

"There is nothing so personal, so important, as a person's name. Tis part of who they are. And so of course I remembered her name," I say.

Aiken sits back in our little corner of the darkened but lively inn, watching me.

"Do you not agree?"

"You are a curious woman, Hilla."

I've been called many things, but never . . . curious.

"Aye?"

"Why did you look at me when the serving maid asked if you cared for more ale?"

Not expecting the question, I think on it for a moment. And realize I'd not have done so before becoming Lady Whitley.

"Habit, I suppose."

Aiken thanks Mistress Coraline as she places a tankard and freshly baked bread onto the table.

"Did he mistreat you?"

My answer is immediate. "Aye."

Aiken's jaw grinds together, as if he cares that I'd been poorly treated by my husband.

"I'd been troubled since our betrothal was announced. No young lady wishes to marry a man of his age or reputation."

"But your father sought an alliance with the border lords?"

"Aye." I drink, remembering that day. "I knew as the future queen of Meria I'd not choose my own husband. Even still, I could not keep the disappointment from my face. Father had been furious with me, but what was I to do? Feign excitement at the prospect?"

I drink again.

"I took no pleasure in being his wife, but neither did I shirk my duties. At least we remained at court. I had Cettina, and my ladies."

I do believe I may be getting drunk.

"And then the affair," he finishes.

"Whitley had been furious, of course. When my father disavowed me, when we were exiled, his anger knew just one restraint. Surprisingly, he never struck me. But for bringing dishonor to his family name, for marrying a disgraced princess instead of the would-be queen . . . I think it may have been easier for me had he beaten me if it could have spared me from all the rest."

Aiken fills both of our mugs.

"Those scars may have healed," I finish lamely, not wishing to detail my confinement. Or the shame of being made to sit with the servants, who resented me as much as their master.

"Why did you not allow your sister to grant you a divorce after the king died?"

"I told you," I start, but he does not accept it.

"To feed her information? I cannot think the queen would allow you to endure such treatment for the purpose of having an informant."

Not wishing to discuss my husband, or my marriage, any longer, I break off a piece of bread.

"You overestimate Cettina's will and underestimate mine."

I look back toward the door as I chew.

"Is that normal, to have someone standing guard. At an inn?"

When he doesn't answer, I look back to my companion. His expression is answer enough. Suddenly, it makes sense.

"You know the innkeeper. You have scouts. That man, he is also in your employ?"

No damned answer. Of course.

"Do all Elderman wield such influence?"

Nothing.

"Or just the Prima's personal guard?"

I could be wrong, but it seems as if Aiken is staring at my lips.

"Fine, you keep your secrets, and I shall keep my own. Stubborn bugger."

The corners of his mouth lift.

"Is that a smile I see? Such a rare sight indeed. A pity that. You are much more handsome when you smile."

His mouth continues to curve upward. A miracle.

"I do believe I am getting drunk," I inform him.

"Shall I take away your ale?"

I intend to keep the conversation light, to force the blasted man to continue to smile. But instead my answer is deadly serious.

"I will unlearn what Whitley has taught me. And will not look to a man for answers on how I should behave."

Amused, he continues to smile. My heart races at the sight.

"A good plan, my lady."

Aiken raises his mug.

"To life."

I've heard the toast before but cannot think of where. I raise my mug to his own. But just before I echo his words, it comes to me.

Aye, I've heard those words before. And they are not words that an Elderman should be uttering.

Tis the toast of the Garra.

13

AIKEN

The lady is indeed drunk, or approaching it. And clearly not accustomed to such a state. And perhaps I've had one too many ales as well, for the look on her face tells me I've made a rare mistake.

"How do you know those words?" she asks, confirming my suspicion.

Putting the mug down and ignoring the meal that is now being placed in front of us, I consider my words carefully.

"I'm surprised you recognize them," I venture, and am immediately struck down.

"Nay, you will not waylay me. How do you know the words? More importantly, why do you, an Elderman, use them?"

The truth would make it much easier to convince Hilla of my plan.

Though the truth, I'm afraid, would frighten her. Thus far, I've told Hilla only part of what I'd learned today. What I neglected to tell her is that the borders are much too dangerous for us to wander near. It seems our pursuers were not the least bit discouraged when we disappeared into this town, in this inn where none who are not recognized can enter, and have indeed redoubled their efforts. We cannot go to Edingham now. Too many men for me to engage with are now camped just a day's ride from us.

We will ride further, into Meria, instead. But Hilla will not take kindly to the fact.

Treading carefully, I tell her a partial truth.

"Once, in a tavern very much like this one, I met a Garra. A direct descendant of Athea."

"It cannot be. The original Garra's descendants have long died out."

"Nay," I correct her, "they have not. When she was blamed for the breakup of the Isle, held responsible for the kingdoms being split into two, it became necessary for her and her kin to go into hiding. Admitting to being a descendant of Athea was dangerous."

"I know all of this," she says. "My mother had an interest in the Garra."

Hence, her awareness of the words I used typically associated with them. Many of the Garra's teachings have made their way into the Isle's culture, but others, like the Kona, a doll that represents Garra beliefs, or that particular Garra toast, have not.

"So you met a healer once and she told you of that phrase?"

To life. For the Garra, love is at the heart of all their beliefs. The consummation of that love, something to be celebrated. And so, another truth . . .

"I confessed my past to this particular healer, knowing there would be no judgment. We forged a connection because of it."

Hilla appears thoughtful.

"My mother taught Cettina and me that a person's worth lies in how they treat themselves, and others. Tis naught to do with the value of their gowns or jewels, their rank. It made Father furious that she insisted we assist in every job in the castle. From the kitchens"—I look toward the barmaid who moves from table to table with efficiency—"to the role of chambermaid."

I rest back in my chair, listening with interest. Hilla's eyes are sharp. Intelligent. And so I can guess her question even before she asks it.

"How do you reconcile the church's beliefs with your own?"

I don't. Which is precisely why this particular mission, as an Elderman, has been the most difficult one I've ever undertaken.

"Within the church, beliefs vary. Some more extreme than others."

She makes a face. "The Prima, you mean?"

"Aye, Father Silvester among them."

"And yet you serve the man, do you not? Shadow Warriors are like his personal guards?"

"They were not always so. We were formed after Edingham was created to protect those who traveled to Avalon to worship. In those days, crossing the border, as we've done, was unheard of. Without escort, at least."

"Hmm. So do you believe the mere act of a woman looking directly into a man's eyes can tempt him into sin, as the church teaches?"

Not before meeting you.

'Twas easier when I thought Hilla a traitor. Who could be tempted by a woman who plots to murder innocents? But this woman. Aye, she could tempt me even if I were an Elderman.

"You look at me now, and I am not tempted into sin," I lie.

She holds my gaze.

"So nay? You do not believe it?"

Leaning forward, my chest pressed against the table in front of me, I continue to stare at her. A most pleasing pastime. "I believe it only as much as the opposite is true."

She blinks, and then understands my meaning.

"I am as tempted by you as you are by me," she says. "Which is to say, not at all."

Clever woman.

Assuming the identity of someone you are not requires vigilance. So I say this to her fully aware that I should not. That Father Aiken would not.

But I am no man of God.

"You, my lady, are a liar."

Her lips part, the truth of my words apparent to us both. I think of the sleepless night I had on the wooden floor, a more comfortable accommodation than many I've had over the years. Made less so by my knowledge of this very woman lying just above me, utterly and completely nude.

I saw nothing of her, with the coverlet pulled up to her chin. But that did not stop my imagination from roaming free.

"I've never known desire before, so perhaps you are right."

With that statement, so casually given, Hilla begins to eat, our moment of flirtation thankfully over. Reminding myself she is both married and a queen's sister, I follow suit. The meat pie as good as yesterday, I remind myself to compliment Nathan.

He's done well for himself here, has made Crow's End one of the most indispensable of all our safe dwellings across the Isle.

And while I've not drunk enough to be caught unaware, my tongue is looser than it should be. *Say little, for doing so will keep you out of trouble.*

This conversation does not qualify as a good model of my training.

"Not even before you wed?" I ask, still curious, though I should not be so.

Hilla puts down her knife and washes down her meal with a sip of ale.

"Not truly. I could not steal innocent kisses like other ladies at court were able to do."

"Interesting."

She shrugs, as if it does not matter. But tis easy enough to see it matters to her a great deal. The Hilla Affair, as it became known, has scarred her deeply.

"Tis so," she admits.

"If you did not do it, how is it you were blamed?"

She hesitates.

"Hilla." I force her to look at me with the force of my tone. "I would never betray you."

But of course, she does not believe that. Nor should she, even if tis true.

"I cannot," she says finally.

I think back to all I know of the incident. So few details. I know only what most others do, that she'd been accused of cuckolding her husband with Lord Bowes, a minor noble. The man was later beheaded, Hilla stripped of her inheritance, and she and Whitley tossed from court.

"Was an innocent man put to death?"

No," she says flatly.

So Bowes did have an affair, but not with Hilla. Interesting.

Just as interesting is the look Nathan gives me from across the room. Tis a look of warning. One I know well.

"Hilla."

She smiles at me. A smile I did not earn.

"We cannot travel east. The borders are teeming with

men from Craighcebor." I hesitate, rubbing the back of my neck. "When I told you before our pursuers were men from Craighcebor, I was not actually so certain then that they were. But I am certain now. And they are hunting you, watching and waiting along the borders."

Her carefree smile flees. "But Cettina's men are looking for me—you said so yourself. They are traveling along the border in search of me too. If we could just find them . . ."

"I cannot guarantee we will do so before you are taken into custody by those who would blame you for the attack. I am but one man."

She considers my words.

"I am due at the Merian court. If you accompany me there, I can guarantee safe passage to Breywood Castle."

Edingham's capital sits along the coast, and it will be easy enough to get her there once at d'Almerita, traveling by sea.

"I am not well loved at Castle d'Almerita."

"Nay," I agree, "but King Galfrid will welcome you just the same. I know him to be an honorable man." I cannot tell her how I know this. "You will be safer in the southwest than you are here, or along the border."

"Will he not simply apprehend me for the attack?"

"He will not," I assure her. "I can promise you that."

If she is confused, there is no hope for it. I cannot say any more.

"I'd not put you in danger."

"And yet you've done so. I was mere moments away from my sister's men."

"A fact I now regret," I say honestly. "But one that does not change our current situation. I want only to keep you safe."

She is confused, but I can do nothing to alleviate it.

"My sister will worry."

A fact I'd already considered.

"I will have word sent to her of your safekeeping."

Light from the candle at the center of the table flickers in her sharp eyes as they narrow. "I will trust you if you'll answer but one question."

Convincing her to change course was easier than I'd expected.

"Go ahead then," I prompt her, eager to know if before first light we will be making our way further west of the border.

"Who are you really, Father Aiken?"

14

HILLA

$\mathcal{B}$eing woken before dawn did not annoy me.

Being made to wear a servant's gown and sleeveless tunic that he'd somehow acquired yesterday in town did not bother me at all. Riding two to a saddle though . . . it was damned uncomfortable. For no other reason than I am more acutely aware of Aiken at my back than I was before we reached Crow's End. There is a difference between the reticent Elderman who'd captured me and the man at my back.

With him no longer wearing robes, I find myself forgetting that he is, indeed, an Elderman. Sword ever-present, and having donned a tunic I've not yet seen him wear, Aiken could pass easily for a commander. He certainly gives orders like one.

"Will we stop soon?"

The sun had risen long ago. After crossing a stream that convinced me we would drown and a mountain Aiken called a "small mound," I am more than ready for my feet to touch flat ground.

"Only when tis necessary. Do you need for us to stop, Hilla?"

Even when he talks, Aiken somehow sounds as if he says few words. How does he manage such a thing?

"Nay," I admit, knowing that because we ride double, our pace will be slow. When I asked how long it would take for us to reach Castle d'Almerita, he replied that it would have taken him a fortnight alone. Clearly it will be longer with us both.

"How far do you think they will follow?"

At least he seemed more inclined to answer my questions than before.

"I do not know."

Turning in the saddle, I see enough of Aiken's face to read his expression.

"You are worried."

"Nay," he lies.

And then looks at me.

When he does that, my stomach twists in knots. If there was ever any man I could not have, it is this one. Laughing at his attempt to quiet me as we made our way to the bedchamber last eve—apparently I giggle when I've had too much ale to drink—I fell asleep with just one thought. And 'twas not for my safety.

Or even, surprisingly, of Cettina. Aiken assured me not only had Whitley been well and truly caught, but that he would not be set free, even without my testimony. He seems assured about many things an Elderman should not have knowledge of, convincing me the question I asked is a good one.

Who is this man, precisely?

Of course, he refused to answer. And I agreed to this plan with little choice despite it.

I turn back just as Aiken swerves us away from a hanging branch. This road, less traveled according to my guide, will at times be overgrown and seem more perilous.

As I did last eve when I lay on the pillow, I consider my own future. Of course I still worry for the threats to Cettina's reign and the kingdom. But my own husband was the most pressing threat these past months, and that, at least, is behind us. But what of me?

"You are unusually quiet."

I smile at the wide-open fields ahead of us. Tis beautiful, a small pond not far away, its glistening water inviting. The sun has fully risen now, and as we travel southwest, tis just slightly warmer. Each day I imagine it will be more so.

"You seem to enjoy the quiet," I respond.

When silence is his answer, I laugh aloud.

"See? You've nothing to say to that even."

He shifts in the saddle, and I move my backside forward to accommodate him. With Aiken's arms around my waist so as to grip the reins, I continually do not know where to lay my hands. So they rest together on the saddle horn in front of me. But many times, as we stumble or gallop, especially downhill, I've reached for the reins as well—and then immediately pulled back, my hands touching his now-ungloved ones.

"I was thinking," I say to fill the silence, "of what will happen when I return home."

Once again, I turn toward him, but Aiken does not answer.

"I will return home, will I not?"

Aiken slows us to a stop. Somehow our position seems less intimate when we are moving. But now, as his mount dances beneath us, the massive warhorse the largest I've ever ridden, our position seems . . . improper.

More so than sleeping in the same chamber with him without any clothing?

"You will return home, Hilla. I vow it on my life."

Shivering despite the sun's warmth, I'm unable to look away. He stares at my lips, and I want, despite everything, for him to kiss me. If he did, I'd likely fall off the horse in horror. But that does not stop me from wanting it.

"I was thinking," I finish, swallowing, "of what it will mean to be wedded to a man arrested for plotting against my sister."

Rarely can I read Aiken's expression. But this time, his eyes clearly say what my mind has already reconciled.

Aiken confirms it.

"You are likely to be a widow before long, Hilla. Mayhap even before you arrive at Breywood."

Before I can stop them, tears spring to my eyes. I'd not let the thought form fully in my mind before now.

I turn before he can see me fully. Wiping my eyes with my fingers, I will them to stop. But they will not.

He leans down into my ear.

"Why do you cry for a man such as him?"

I shake my head, unable to say the words. And still, the tears come.

Please stop.

But they will not listen.

"Hilla?"

I bow my head, remembering he is, after all, an Elderman.

"Forgive me," I choke out between tears. "Forgive me," I repeat.

His hands are now on my shoulders. Squeezing gently, reassuringly.

"Hilla?"

I shake my head again. This time, he will not be refused.

His fingers grab my chin and guide my head to turn toward him.

But Aiken's eyes do not judge. There is no censure there for the thoughts running through my head, ones I wish would flee and never return. Instead, only understanding.

"I wish the bastard dead too," he says.

15

AIKEN

"*D*o not move."

I've traveled this way twice before, and it seemed a good place to stop. Though the running water nearby could attract others, the site is far off the main road.

But now someone is coming.

I point to the thicket we just crossed, a finger to my lips.

She hears nothing, but Hilla is not trained for this. Turning my head toward the wind to confirm my suspicions, I slowly unsheathe my sword. They are closer than I would like. At least two or three men.

Though I can tell Hilla is scared, I can do nothing to reassure her. The element of surprise is the only advantage we have. I make my way to the thickest tree trunk and position myself so as not to be seen. Sure enough, moments later, the sounds of approaching horses are evident even to Hilla, who watches me, still holding Sorel's reins. She likes the lady, thankfully.

As do I.

Peeling my eyes from Hilla and Sorel, one of the many

gifts Baldric gave to me, I wait as the riders approach. Three men. Separating them is my only chance.

When the first man passes, I do nothing. Thankfully, the third one is further behind, so when I move from my position to get between him and the others, I do not give his companions a chance to come to my target's rescue. Before he or his mount are alerted to my presence, I reach up and grab his leg, yanking him off his horse, though he manages to stumble to his feet.

My sword is at his throat before he can raise an alarm.

The moment his companions realize what has happened, they spin toward us.

"Weapons," I shout.

I tighten my grip, twisting my captive's arm in a way that fells him to the ground. Craning to look over my shoulder, I'm quick to shift my focus to the other men. If you give a person the chance to think, they will. I cannot afford the reivers the opportunity to do so.

"Now."

Both men, stupidly, draw and drop their swords.

"Dismount," I order, my sword still at the man's throat, his head pulled back due to my fistful of his hair. As they do, I pray my hunch is correct.

Their hobblers and padded gambesons mark them border reivers. But they could still pose a threat to Hilla if they'd been ordered to find her.

"Who are you?"

The man at the lead answers, eyeing me warily.

"Naught but reivers. We travel to Sindridge."

Ahh. Wine smugglers.

"You are from Edingham, then?"

The man whose hair I currently grip nods.

Looking for evidence of their claim, something that

would not make them a threat to Hilla, I find it in their speech. Their dress. But one mystery remains.

"You have no cart for transporting."

They are surprised I've devised their occupation so quickly.

"There are others, a half day's ride ahead."

Also not surprising as reivers typically travel in packs.

When I let go, reaching for the man's collar and lifting him to his feet, he glares at me but says nothing.

Sheathing my sword, I reach out my hand to shake his, not wanting enemies on this road.

"I am but one man traveling with my wife," I say by way of explanation. He looks at it for a moment, and then takes it. His grip around my wrist marks the man a Highlander. When he lets go, I take a risk, but one that will keep Hilla and I safe from these reivers.

Laying my sword on the ground in front of me, though close enough for me to grab, I wait for his reaction.

It is a particular custom of the Highlands, one that leaves a man completely vulnerable. Hilla gasps, but I ignore her. Instead, I wait for the man, a fully bearded one who has seen at least forty summers, to lean down and take my sword.

Handing it to me, he leaves me to sheathe it as he turns back to grab the reins of his mount. By the time we make our way to Hilla, the men have begun to speak again. An understanding between us.

Introducing myself as a minor border lord on his way to find a Garra reputed to be near the town of Reiner, my "wife" Lady Julie stands by, silently watching us. If Hilla is surprised by the reason I give for our travel, she does not show it.

In fact, she aids in my desire to make the men uneasy enough to avoid asking further questions. Not one of the men make eye contact with me or my "wife" after that announcement. Speaking of such matters aloud is absurdly frowned upon. Tis no less objectionable to discuss the Garra so openly. Garra are more accepted in large cities and in places such as Murwood End, but in many, they are relegated to the far-flung edges of society.

She rubs her stomach.

"We are unable to conceive a child," she says.

Not one of the men make eye contact with me or my "wife" after that announcement.

With that, the leader of the reivers looks to our fire.

"If you've a mind to share it, we've fresh fowl to offer."

I'd noticed the kills hanging from his mount.

Hilla and I exchange a glance. At my nod, she welcomes the three men as if they were courtiers and she, the queen. She orders each of us to move rocks and logs, and by the time the men's horses are fed and watered, the very same man whose throat was in danger of being slashed not long ago sits beside me as we clean our supper.

"How did you do it?" their leader asks me, referring to the way I took down his friend.

Convincing them we are no danger to them after my maneuver is not an easy task.

"An elder in our village taught me that trick," I say, attempting to dismiss the question.

He eyes me with more suspicion than I'd care for. Mayhap it was a mistake to agree to share the fire, but doing otherwise would not have endeared the men to us. With three here and likely the same number, or more, ahead of us, I've no desire to deal with reivers in addition to those hunting down Hilla.

Were I alone, I'd have outrun these reivers already.

We need another mount. I'll not survive the journey with Hilla's bottom squirming in front of me, and we will be quicker. Unfortunately, none were to be had in Rimstead.

By the time we eat, the men seem to have forgotten our

wayward greeting. Thankfully, their leader confirms what I'd hoped. After the meal, they will be leaving. Reivers most often travel at night, these men no exception.

Their crude humor does not appear to bother Hilla. She addresses them with ease. Laughs at their jests. Does more than I could have on my own to convince the men we're naught but a man and his wife. No further threat to them.

Until the leader says to Hilla and me, "If you didn't put so much space between you, a babe might result."

They all laugh, but his words are duly noted. If Hilla and I are not acting as if we are indeed husband and wife, there is good reason. But the risk to us is too great were these men to develop suspicions about us. Moving closer, at a break in the conversation, I whisper into my "wife's" ear.

"I am going to kiss you."

Hilla near falls off the log in a fit of coughing. Not a reaction I'd expected. When she finishes, all three of the men look at us.

"Are you well?" I ask.

But that is not the question, and Hilla knows it. I seek her permission for something else.

"Aye, well enough now. Thank you, husband."

Now is my chance.

16

HILLA

*T*is not a sin to want to save our lives.

Even before their jest, I wondered if the men had noticed Aiken and I do not touch. Shamelessly, the thought came to me as an excuse to move closer to him. Surely man and wife would be more at ease with each other?

I'm fooling no one—not God nor myself. As Aiken leans into me, I want this even though I should not. But if he deems it necessary for the ruse, why should I argue? He'd not break such a sacred vow if our lives were not in danger.

At the first touch of his lips, I nearly come off the log, so charged is the touch. His lips are soft, and warm. They cover mine so perfectly. Aiken's hand cups my cheek as the men clap and howl. How could the same person who came so close to slitting a man's throat be so gentle now?

And then, his lips are gone.

Except that I could feel them for long after Aiken and the reivers resumed their conversation. I do not contribute, or even listen, as I'd done before. Instead, I resist the urge to touch my lips where his had been.

If I'd known it would feel that way. If I'd known flutters

would begin in my chest and travel down to my very core. If I'd known a simple touch as that could warm my cheeks, my chest, my whole body, in a way the fire in front of us could never have done.

I might very well have had the damn affair I'd been accused of.

Nay, Hilla. You would not.

'Twould have disappointed my mother. And my sister. And God. But most of all, myself. I know that because even now I feel poorly for wanting Aiken's kiss so badly.

"My lady?"

One of the men must have asked me a question.

As Aiken slips his fingers through mine, his hand clasping around me like an anchor, my "husband" repeats the question.

"He asked, 'Would you like more meat?'"

Clearly, Aiken was not affected as I'd been by that kiss.

"Nay," I say, marveling at the ease with which our hands intertwine. I have never held the hand of a man before now. Not once. And it is wholly unlike any other feeling. Tis as if . . .

"We leave you to your fire then."

One by one, each of the men stand. Unfortunately, Aiken does as well. Our contact, broken. I do not move. Or speak. It is not until their saddlebags are repacked and Aiken calls to me that I stand.

"Fare thee well, my lady," says the very man Aiken assaulted. The one who could have killed him had he not accepted the sword at his feet. 'Twas a dangerous thing to do, and though I've not seen it before, I have heard of the Highlander custom.

"Fare thee well."

Oddly, bidding adieu to a reiver in the middle of the woods halfway between the borders and the capital of Meria is not even the most remarkable of circumstances I've found myself in this past sennight.

Being dragged by my husband and his men to Craighcebor, not knowing precisely what they planned but being thrust into a horrific plot . . . lying naked in the same chamber as an Elderman, a handsome one at that, who'd taken me against my will . . .

"Are you well?"

I'm broken out of my reverie by that very man now.

"Tis all just so . . ." I have no words to explain. "I do not know whose life I live now."

As I talk, Aiken makes his way back to the fire, and I join him. This time, on a separate log. Though I can still feel his lips on mine. His fingers intertwined with my own.

"You could have been killed. I could have been killed," I say.

He does not seem bothered.

"When you laid your sword on the ground . . ."

Aiken picks up the long stick in front of him that he'd been using to stoke the fire. "'Twas a risk, aye. But the bigger risk would have been allowing those men, and the others in the party ahead of us, to see me as their enemy."

I open my mouth to ask why he had not simply greeted the newcomers rather than attack them, but the words do not come out. Instead, I find myself staring at his lips. Remembering.

"I apologize for kissing you," he says, somehow guessing my thoughts. "I should have realized their suspicions earlier."

"'Twas necessary. No need to apologize."

"And I am sorry for taking you, Hilla. And for the treatment you will endure these weeks on the road. Sleeping on the ground, fearing for your safety. I am sorry for it."

Though I'm unsure what brought this turnabout in Aiken, tis a welcome apology.

"You protected my sister, so I thank you for that. Though still, I do not know why."

He says nothing. And I know by now whatever secrets Aiken keeps, they are not ones he will share with me.

"May I propose," he says, sitting back down as the fire rages, "a truce? I will not inquire as to the true story of how you lost your crown. And you will do the same as to my motivation for protecting your sister."

I like this Aiken, the one who talks.

"Or with regard to your apparent distaste for the man you serve?" I add. "Or the network of men you seem to have?" I ask, thinking of his scouts and the innkeeper of Crow's End. "Or why," I venture, as boldly as my sister might, "you look at me in such a way even though you have taken a vow of celibacy?"

As soon as the words leave my mouth, I regret them. Truly, why did I ask such a question? The events of the past few days have caused me to take leave of my senses.

Aiken leans forward, resting his elbows on both knees.

We are further apart than before, but not so far apart that, with the firelight so close by, I cannot see his eyes. His lips may not be upturned, but a faint smile is there nonetheless, making me glad, and not ashamed, I'd asked the question.

"Answering the first question could put me in danger. The second, even more so. As to the third . . ." He pauses. As always, Aiken is measuring his answer. Will it be that of a stranger, polite and meaningless? Or will he answer in truth?

"Tis the most dangerous question of all."

17

AIKEN

*J*olted awake by a hawk's cry, Hilla sits up in the saddle. She's slumbered against my chest often these past fifteen days. Our pace has been punishing, so I'm glad for it. If there were other ways I could atone for the fact that she's been put in danger, I would do it.

Knowing her as I do now after more than a sennight, the thought of her plotting with Whitley against her sister is beyond absurd. The opposite, in fact, is true.

Hilla lives to serve her sister.

At first I believed it was guilt for having inadvertently thrust Cettina into her role as queen of Edingham. But each night as we sit beside the fire, or twice since Crow's End at a table inside an inn, I learn a bit more.

In part because of her nature, and in part as the older sister, Hilla has clearly been attending to Cettina for many years. I suspect the death of their mother plays a part as well.

"How long did I sleep?" she asks, turning in the saddle.

As ever, I'm struck by the ease at which she's taken to this journey. A woman raised to be queen, and yet she's not once complained about the lack of a bed. She's laundered her own gown, even learned how to skin a rabbit. A task I'd been surprised Hilla wanted to learn.

"Not long."

She turns back and sits up in the saddle, and looks around us. There is nothing to see now, but beyond the ridge in front of us . . . I look forward to her reaction at seeing d'Almerita. The walled town, host to Castle d'Almerita and the capital of Meria, is not far from us.

Resting back against me, she says nothing. We ride in companionable silence, and I wait. She's seen d'Almerita before, but with a child's eyes. Mayhap she will not be as awestruck as I was when Baldric and I first climbed this ridge. For a boy who'd never left his home, it had been a remarkable sight indeed. I can easily recall my feelings from that day.

Hope. Trepidation. Wonder.

Saved from the streets and brought to the greatest town in all the Isle. That boy had been scared too, but not for long. Not three years later I returned from a visit to my mother an entirely different person. No longer a boy of ten and nine but a man who'd learned how to never be afraid again.

"Oh my."

Indeed.

Even from this distance, the blues of the Merian Sea glitter behind the walled town, Castle d'Almerita rising high above the other buildings.

"Tis beautiful." Hilla leans forward. "So much more than I remember."

Although her own home is as spectacular in some ways, the colors here, oranges and reds and whitewashed stone, are very different than in Edingham. As we traveled south, the days have become warmer and warmer. Flowers that could be found here alone bloom all around us.

From this distance, the turmoil Meria now faces is hidden.

"You are sure about this?" she asks.

Unlike these past weeks, I've many allies in Meria. Baldric's son among them.

"Aye," I reassure her as we move once more, confident in the well-defined plan. "You will be safe here, Hilla."

Last eve she bathed in the lake near where we stayed. Resisting the temptation to go to her, to be assured she was safe even though none were close by—indeed we never did see reivers again, or the men from Craighcebor—I finally convinced myself the desire was a selfish one.

And not the first selfish thought I'd had these past days.

Riding with her. Sleeping near her. I'm ready for this torture to end. No stranger to women, both before and after I was recruited, although not since I took my "vows," tis plain enough I need to put distance between myself and this particular woman.

Another man's wife.

Hilla refuses to be presented to the king in "such a state" and I need information, so as we ride into the city gates, I steer us toward another inn rather than the castle. Protocol forbids strangers here, but there is no help for it. Circumstances force us through the winding streets into an alley more well-preserved than some main roads in other towns.

When we reach the back of the building and dismount, I tie my horse to a post.

"Why do we wait? I thought you mentioned a tavern?"

Even though we are on the outskirts of town, too many people mill about. Hilla peeks over my shoulder to the sea in the distance. No wall separates the water and d'Almerita here. The cliffs beyond us are a natural barrier all along the coast.

"Back to not speaking," she mutters.

I smile inwardly. Silence unsettles Hilla.

As the lone straggler leaves our alley, I knock four times in quick succession, followed by a fifth knock.

After a peephole opens, and then promptly closes, the door swings open I grab Hilla's arm and pull her inside.

Although it appears as any other tavern, Ale and Bedde is anything but.

"Come with me."

Weaving through tables of men who do not glance at us, men as trained as I am to see without seeing, I steer us to a set of stairs in the back. Climbing them, my heart pounding in my chest for having Hilla in here, knowing I've no other choice, we make our way to the end of the corridor.

And here, we wait.

"Aiken? What is this place? What do we wait for?"

"Who is she and why is she here?"

We both turn toward the sound of the deep voice.

"I'm surprised it took you this long," I say to the new arrival. Hilla looks back and forth between us.

Although he's seen more than seventy summers, our new companion stands tall, nearly as tall as I. His hair is now completely white, his bearing as regal as ever.

"Lady Hilla," I answer. "Sister to the Queen of Edingham."

In all these years, I've never been able to surprise him as I've done this day.

"Hilla," I say, "this is Lord Baldric Orazio."

My mentor. My savior.

And one extremely angry man.

"YOU SHOULD NOT HAVE BROUGHT HER HERE."

Baldric and I sit in the corner of the small hall. Hilla has left us to wash up after our long journey. Within minutes of meeting her, Baldric arranged for a bath, a meal and a gown. If need be, the man could summon a ship from Murwood End. A Garra from the heart of the Highlands. In some ways, he is more powerful than the king himself.

"Where," I ask, "would you have had me bring her? Directly to court after so many days of travel? Before I know that it's safe?"

Baldric, who's been frowning since we came, does not relent. "You could have sent word."

"Aye," I agree. "I could have."

He would be less pleased to hear my reasons for not doing so. I'm certain Baldric would not consider Hilla's comfort a reason to put off another delay. So I use another.

"Silvester will become suspicious if I am gone too long. Is he in d'Almerita yet?"

Although we are separated from others, and both Baldric and I trust every man, and woman, in this establishment, not all know of my current assignment. Indeed, had I appeared in my robes it would have caused a stir. One Baldric would clearly like to avoid.

"He's here."

Finally, we move on from Hilla.

"Tell me."

Baldric clearly wishes to berate me further over Hilla. But

he is pragmatic, more so than most. So instead, he forges ahead after taking a large swig of ale.

"He meets with the king in three days' time. But none are hopeful of the outcome. While you've been gone, Hinton's supporters have grown bold."

After the king publicly refused to name his nephew as heir, Lord Hinton made no secret of his intention to fight his uncle for the throne. In the weeks that passed since I've been attempting to quell the unrest at the border, under the guise of supporting it, it seems matters have not improved.

"He is a fool."

Father Silvester already showed his hand by meeting so publicly with Hinton. Whatever his demands, King Galfrid will have none of it.

The die has been cast. Tis only to be made formal, Galfrid's break with the head of the church. And then, war.

"No less so than Hinton. Tell me of the princess."

I recount everything since I'd last spoken to Baldric. Of the Tournament of Loigh and the meeting to which Silvester sent me, the one Lord Whitley himself attended which alerted me to his plan. I tell him of my alliance with Queen Cettina's commander, Lord Stokerton. And of Craighcebor. I end with the current situation that sees Lady Hilla abovestairs in a place that no one but its members should be allowed to enter.

"Had you not been at that meeting . . ." He stops, considering. "Silvester is becoming reckless."

The Prima, who had come from humble beginnings, has grown more and more influential throughout the years. While King Galfrid simply tolerated him, Cettina's father encouraged a stronger alliance that saw the church's influence in Edingham grow.

But now he seeks to take advantage of the instability of both kingdoms—the Borderers and some Highlanders in

Edingham still calling for war over the attack that never came to pass when the Oryan sank—and Galfrid's succession crisis. But in doing so, and sending me to treat with the very men that would have seen innocents killed to reach their goal, he has gone too far.

"Do we tell the king of Father Silvester's involvement?"

He asks the same question I'd been considering for days. When I left Avalon for the Tournament of Loigh, Silvester had been clear. Recruit the Highlanders to our cause by any means necessary. He would, of course, deny any cantonment of innocent men and women to achieve such means.

"What do you think?" I ask.

As always, Baldric has an answer. "If you do, you will be outed. At a time when we need to know Silvester's every move."

"Galfrid will tell his Curia," I agree. "From there, I am on borrowed time."

"Aye."

"Although I do not see any other way," I say. "Perhaps we can speak to Roger first."

It would be difficult to gain a private audience with Baldric's son, a member of the king's Curia, once Hilla's presence at court is known.

"Aye. Bring the princess to Galfrid, speak to Roger and decide. But remember the oath."

As if I could forget.

Finishing his ale, the elusive Lord Orazio sits back and contemplates this turn of events.

"My lord?" One of Baldric's many runners approaches, handing him a large package.

"Give it to him."

I've seen the young man before, but his name eludes me. About to ask it, the boy shoves the package at me, bows and hurries away.

Bristling at Baldric's laugh, I down the remainder of ale and stand.

"Your reputation precedes you, Aiken."

"What did you tell him about me? The poor boy was terrified."

By his dark tan belt, I can see the runner is in his very early stages of training.

Baldric smiles, his mood much improved.

"Just the truth."

18

HILLA

$\mathcal{A}$lthough my hands tremble as we prepare to walk through the ornate doors that lead to King Galfrid's private solar chamber, I know how to feign calm. My father had become a spiteful, mean old man as he aged, but there was a time, when Mother was alive, that he had been tolerable. And wise. I'd learned much from him.

If only we could have taken the best of him as a leader, and father, and rid him of all the hate and bitterness. He'd have told me now to breathe deeply, ensure my shoulders are not tense, and above all, make and maintain eye contact with the king.

Which it seems I will have the opportunity to do as two footmen step forward to open the doors. Aiken, once again wearing his robes, lowers his cowl. I suppose it is good he was able to gain an audience this eve, giving me less time to think about this meeting. No matter his assurances that all will be well, the man sitting on the throne is my enemy.

The chamber's riches are at odds with his lack of a crown. Indeed, the aging king could be any other man except he sits at the center of the others. And his bearing clearly marks him as their leader.

Both his hair, and beard, are a mixture of dark grey and white. Regal and discerning, he watches as I enter the room. Bowing, his station above mine, I wait for longer than necessary to rise.

When I do, the king looks at me. I do not flinch.

How Aiken's man procured this gown, a perfectly fitting light blue and silver creation, so quickly, or even how he gained this audience the very night of our arrival, I do not know.

Since we came to d'Almerita, Aiken has been more like the man I first met than my companion of this past fortnight. Gone was the relaxed man who had been open to talking and sharing or even smiling, replaced by the man of silence and mystery. That establishment he took us to, the Ale and Bedde, was no less an enigma, unlike any inn we visited along the way, and despite how many times I asked about that strange place, it remained yet as mysterious as my companion.

There was little to complain about with my bath at the inn, however. Though the wooden tub was smaller than most, after so many days on the road, it was most luxurious and most welcome. Then a lady's maid appeared from nowhere to dress my hair and offer the perfectly fitted gown I wear now. At the height of fashion, its sleeves are long and as low as its neckline, its silver-belted chain glittering with blue gems that match the gown itself.

"Princess, welcome to Castle d'Almerita."

"My thanks, King Galfrid. It has been many years since we've met. I am sorry for your loss."

He nods but says nothing of the loss of his son as his onlookers watch the exchange. "Many rumors swirl upon your arrival. Tell me how you've come to be here."

As he's known for his bluntness, the question does not surprise me.

"My husband, Lord Whitley, had planned to attack your border village of Craighcebor. He and his allies continue to press my sister for war against Meria as retaliation for Oryan," I say, equally as blunt. "I had no choice but to accompany him, which is where Father Aiken—" pausing, I look at Aiken, who knows what I plan to say, "—found me."

"Found you?" asks one of the king's Curia. A commander by the looks of him.

"May I be permitted to address you and your king, Lord d'Abella?" Aiken says, stepping forward.

"Greetings, Father Aiken," this Lord d'Abella says. "Aye, you may."

The king turns his attention to Aiken, who opens his mouth to speak, glances quickly at me, and then closes it.

He knows Aiken. The glimmer of recognition is unmistakable. But, oddly, he addresses him as one would a stranger.

"I found myself in Craighcebor, circumstances beyond my or the lady's control having thrown us together. Fearing for her safety from those who may not separate her husband's deeds and her own, we came here."

Aiken holds back the truth, that he abducted me. It would not serve my cause to plant the same seed of doubt that Aiken initially had with regard to my involvement. The ease with which the Elderman lies is one of many qualities these past days I've had difficulty reconciling Aiken as a man of God.

Such as the way he looks at me, especially.

"We request safe passage to Breywood for Lady Hilla," he finishes.

The king clearly has many questions. But instead of asking them, he leans forward.

"You've my protection while you remain at d'Almerita, Lady Hilla."

"Many thanks, King Galfrid," I say, offering a deep curtsy. If he would offer his protection, I will use the opportunity to further my sister's goal of peace between our kingdoms. I'd expected his skepticism about my motives, but instead he seems content to take Aiken at his word.

"And of course"—he inclines his head slightly to acknowledge my silent offer of a temporary truce—"safe passage to Breywood."

He looks at one of the other men beside him.

"Ren, see to the lady's comforts."

And then to me.

"We will meet again tomorrow?"

I curtsy again, thankful for the opportunity but confused at how easily he's accepted our story.

"I look forward to it, my liege."

The man named Ren waits for me just as the king stops Aiken.

"I would speak to you, Father."

Aiken darts a quick glance at me as I allow Ren to escort me from the chamber. More convinced now than ever that there is more to Aiken than I've been led to believe, I leave with the knowledge that, before this night is over, the Elderman *will* provide answers.

AIKEN

*A*s the chamber doors close behind Hilla, the commander approaches, giving me his hand. Shaking it, I'm surprised to see Galfrid standing to approach us as well.

"Well met, my friend," d'Abella says. "I do hope you will be in the capital long enough to finally settle our contest of skills."

The last time I'd stayed here at Castle d'Almerita, the commander and I challenged each other during his visit, his skills with the sword renown. He defeated me the first day. And I him, on the second. We agreed on a rematch when I next returned.

Exchanging a glance with Baldric's son Roger, I nod, just barely, as King Galfrid extends his hand to me. I reach out with my own, unsurprised his grip is so strong.

"We've much to discuss this night," I start, fully cognizant of Roger's continued attempt to assess my motives. I'd have spoken to him first but had been brought to the king the moment I announced Lady Hilla's presence to gain this audience with His Majesty.

"Come." The king leads us to a large circular table in the corner of the chamber. "Sit, and explain how you came to be at the tournament at the behest of the Prima but are here now after warning my men of an attack. Vanni offered few details," he admits.

I sit and catch Roger's eye again.

He shakes his head.

The king, and Vanni, believe me to be Silvester's man. But more important is the oath. That no living man or woman should learn the truth unless lives will be lost in keeping our secret. A tricky thing, determining whether or not a life is truly at risk.

I open my mouth to explain when Roger interrupts.

"The princess," he asks. "What have you learned from her?"

Galfrid looks between us, clearly confused by his man's behavior. When the king asks a question, an answer is expected. But I bide my time, answering Roger first. He is delaying, making certain this is the correct move. The king knows of Baldric, and the Legion, but not of my true identity. Lord d'Abella knows neither. Are Roger and I breaking the oath by telling them?

Nay, I do not believe so. Not with the kingdom in peril if Hinton is not defeated.

"I've learned," I say honestly, "she has no love for her husband. She'd been forced to travel with him to Craighcebor and was glad he had been caught."

At my words, all three men stiffen. An uncomfortable silence fills the air. Do they question her loyalty to Whitley? Our travel had been slow, so word of the attack had already reached them before we arrived. Had the whispers of her potential involvement reached them as well?

"I will not allow Lady Hilla's name to be disparaged any further," I say as sternly as I'm able in the presence of the king. "She had no foreknowledge of the attack and, in fact, had been feeding information to her sister against him. I believe," I say, leaning forward in my seat, "tis as they say. Queen Cettina desires peace with Meria. This attack on Craighcebor was instigated by traitors to the Kingdom of Edingham. The fact that Queen Cettina's men defended a Merian village and thwarted the attack proves they do not conspire against you, King Galfrid. The princess simply has the misfortune of being married to a detestable man who is a traitor to his own queen."

"Father Aiken," d'Abella interrupts, but I continue. If the king believes Hilla guilty of conspiring with her husband, it will not go well for her. "You will remember she had no choice on the marriage. I learned much of her on our journey here." I cannot say anything further without breaking Hilla's confidence. But I will not have the king thinking poorly of a woman who is guilty of nothing more than loyalty to her sister.

"Aiken," Roger says, drawing the attention of both d'Abella and the king. Galfrid knows I am no Elderman, but the commander does not. The pretense of my title dropped, my longtime friend, and brother-in-arms, ignores the others and addresses me alone. "Hilla is not married to a traitor any longer."

I look between him and the others, not understanding.

"Lord Whitley is dead," d'Abella says.

His words are like the point of a sword finding its mark. "Dead?"

"Aye," Roger says. "He was promptly tried and convicted of treason. Executed that very same day. A merchant sailing from Galmouth Bay brought the news two days past."

The chamber grows silent. Tis the very bay in which the Oryan was set to land. If they'd done so it would have been one of the largest attacks on Edingham in recent years. Instead, the ship sank, and with it, Galfrid's son and heir.

Whitley is dead. Hilla, a widow.

I look to the king.

"Is this merchant to be believed? I've heard no rumors of this since arriving."

News such as the execution of Queen Cettina's brother-in-law would have spread wide and fast. Baldric should have heard of it.

The king hesitates.

Roger answers.

"He was no ordinary merchant. I believe," he says, looking around the table, his gaze resting with the king, "it is time for you to learn Father Aiken's true identity."

He darts a look to Vanni, and then back to me.

I nod.

"And for you, Vanni d'Abella, my old friend, to be brought into the fold."

20

HILLA

"I'm here to escort you to the hall, my lady," a chambermaid says, opening the door to my bedchamber.

Since arriving at Castle d'Almerita, I've been offered every comfort imaginable in this beautiful setting. Further south, the colors are brighter, so many reds and oranges that it's difficult not to smile as you walk through the gardens, a view of the Merian Sea nearly around every corner.

I've not seen Aiken since arriving last eve, nor have I spoken to the king. He did, however, send a lady's maid to me, who has offered me the opportunity to dine in the hall this eve, where I am bound to see them both.

But I have not been left to sit bored and idle since I left the king's solar last eve. Earlier today I enjoyed a tour of the grounds by the castle's seneschal himself. Throughout the tour, whispers and stolen glances followed me everywhere, even as I tried to ignore them. . . .

Just a year ago, I'd have had a different reception here. Before the attack on Saitford and the Oryan's sinking, tensions remained as high as they had throughout the Isle's long history, since the kingdoms split. Even so, when Cettina, and my father before her, had treated with the king's representatives, they had been cordial.

And then, the attack on Saitford changed everything.

Now, I am an enemy to the Merians. And anxious to leave this place to return home.

"I will escort the lady."

I freeze at the voice coming from behind the maid.

Aiken.

"Very good, Father."

He steps inside, not hiding his appraisal of me.

Another gown had appeared this morn, the most beautiful one yet. It came with no note, nor explanation. But the maid seemed to know of its presence. She made her way to the trunk and immediately, as the sun rose, began to assist me in preparing for the day.

Like many of the gowns here, it is a lighter shade than I am accustomed to wearing. A pale-yellow silk surcoat over the finest cream linen I've ever worn. Whoever procured this gown was wealthy indeed. The king, I assume? A most-kind gesture given our relationship.

"You look . . . lovely."

"A compliment. Why, thank you, Father," I say, pretending my heart doesn't speed up at his words.

Aiken wears his robes, as expected, his cowl lowered, although something is not quite right. Tis the absence of his sword.

Aiken's jaw ticks at my words. As ever, it seems to annoy him when I use his title.

"A gift from the king, I presume," I say, lifting the fine material up for his inspection. "I will admit to some surprise at my reception."

Aiken doesn't react to that.

"I would speak to you before supper, Hilla."

When he closes the door behind him, I marvel at how natural it feels to be alone with him in this chamber. Such a thing could cause a scandal, another of which I've no desire to be involved in. And yet, I've slept next to him, alone, for many nights. This hardly feels as shocking as it should.

Were he not an Elderman, perhaps. But I've no mind to give the minor impropriety another thought.

"Did your meeting with the king not go well?" I venture. "I had hoped to speak with him today."

Aiken says nothing. He stands so close now I can smell fresh lemon. The scent seems to be a popular one here in d'Almerita. My own soap was scented with it as well.

"Whitley is dead."

I blink, misunderstanding surely.

"Tried, found guilty of treason, executed."

My whole body tingles, from my shoulders down my arms and into my toes.

"A trusted source brought the news to the king just days ago."

I try to ask him for more information, but no words come from me.

"The king bade the man and those who traveled with him to keep the news to themselves. He believes it will embolden his nephew and complicate his upcoming meeting with Silvester."

My husband is dead.

I'm not able to process the political ramifications. Instead, I remember his poor treatment of me. His rage at my supposed affair. Of him coming to my bed, using my body to attempt to produce an heir. I think of the prison that had been my home. And my knees buckle under me.

My chest swells with relief as Aiken holds me upright. Tossing my arms around his shoulders, I allow the tears to flow freely. Gasping for air, I soak the shoulder of his robe, unable to stop. Neither does Aiken pull away, which is just as well as I'd never be able to stand on my own.

"Dead." I do try to pull away now as guilt takes hold of me. "Dead, and I weep with happiness," I chastise myself.

But Aiken will not allow me to wrest free. Instead, he continues to hold me until the tears begin to ebb. A cloth appears in my hands, and I wipe my face with it, pulling back just slightly.

His face, just inches from me.

"Do not feel sorrow for your relief, Hilla. He deserved to die, and your sister saw to it swiftly."

The fact does not surprise me. He'd been caught attempting to kill innocent people to cause a war. If there was ever a treasonable offense, 'twas his. And Cettina would seek to make an example of him to the others who cry for war with Meria. Given his history, and his mistreatment of both me and his position as a border lord, of course she had him hanged.

"Will you pray for my soul, Aiken? That I should be so shameful as to rejoice at my husband's death?"

I stare at his lips as they part. Aiken pauses, as if hesitant. But he does not pull away as I fear he might.

"I will pray for us both, Hilla," he says as his head leans toward mine.

21

AIKEN

You are an Elderman to her.

I jump back, the memory of Hilla's lips on mine, even though it was a farce, never far from my mind. I'd been about to kiss her again in a misguided attempt to comfort her. But this time, for no other reason than I desire it.

A desire that has gotten stronger each day we are together.

"I'm sorry," I say now. Having her in my arms, consoling her—it had almost felt the most natural thing in the world. To kiss her, soothe her tortured soul by making her forget . . . what had I been thinking? "I will get the maid to escort you."

I turn to leave.

Hilla's hand on my arm stops me.

"Nay, Aiken. Stop."

Her face, still streaked with tears, is as lovely as ever.

"You must still have . . . urges. Even though you've pledged yourself to God."

Urges. If only Hilla knew the urges I've had nearly every

night of this journey. It was easier when I thought her a traitor.

"Aye," I agree feebly.

"How could I fault you for such a thing as you stand before me, pardoning me for the joy I feel at Whitley's death?"

"You need not be pardoned, Hilla."

"Then certainly you do not either. Please, stay. Tell me of your meeting with the king. Of what you learned today."

Marveling at how close I came to kissing her, I take a deep breath, attempting to regain control. "I learned of Whitley, of course." And silently rejoiced then, and now, at the news. "And of the king's troubles, which are many."

"Lord Hinton's name has reached even my ears."

"'Tis but a matter of time before he attempts to wrest control of the crown. The king meets with Father Silvester on the morrow."

"Silvester will support Hinton," she says, wise to the situation having lived most of her life at court.

"Indeed, most expect so."

"Which means Meria will be openly at odds with the church?"

"Aye."

"What will happen then?"

All of what I've told her is common knowledge here in d'Almerita. Facts she could learn by speaking to most anyone. Her maid, for instance. Beyond that, I cannot share additional information.

"We shall see," I say, evading the question. "Do you still wish to take supper in the hall?"

Hilla waits for me to say more, realizes I will not, and moves to the basin of water by her bed. Splashing her face with it, careful not to wet her gown, she dries it with the cloth I gave her and places it next to the basin.

With an exchanged glance, of regret and something more, we leave the chamber and make our way through the corridors to the great hall, where supper is well underway.

Of all the great halls on the Isle, from Hilla's home in Edingham to those few castles in Murwood End, none compare to the splendor of this one. Tapestry after tapestry, each one more colorful than the last, lining every bit of space on the stone walls, telling the story of Meria . . . ladies' gowns made of silk . . . gold embellishments everywhere . . . nowhere on the Isle is the gilded history more evident than the court of Castle d'Almerita.

"Tis lovely," Hilla whispers beside me. "Even more so than I remembered."

As we enter, all eyes are on my companion. Many out of curiosity. Hosting a princess of Edingham is not a regular occurrence for those who make the capital their home. No less than fifty people grace the hall, the king not in attendance, it seems, as a servant approaches us.

"This way, my lady. Father."

We're escorted to a long trestle table positioned just beneath the raised dais, which sits empty this eve.

Not surprisingly, the men with whom I've spent the majority of my time here at court are already seated at the same table. I introduce each to Hilla as we sit.

"You'll recognize members of the king's Curia already. Lord Roger Orazio."

Roger inclines his head.

"And next to him, Lord Vanni d'Abella and his wife, Lady Aedre."

I continue introducing the others at our table. As I do, I notice Lady Aedre watching Hilla rather intently.

Just before leaving for the Tournament of Loigh to do Silvester's bidding, I met the Garra—not yet Lady d'Abella—for the first time at Murwood End.

There had been some talk among the Legion of bringing her into the fold, but none could justify it while keeping their oath. But now that her husband is among the very few outsiders that are aware . . .

Throughout the meal, I say little and glance at Hilla even less. Still mortified at what I'd almost done, not for breaking a vow I had not taken, but for telling a woman she had just become a widow and then, mere seconds later, attempting to take advantage of her pain.

The meal passes without incident as I consider how best to appease Silvester on the morrow. He'll know it has been two days since I arrived at the capital. I'd planned to go to him today but worried I'd have been forced to remain at his side, and there had been much to do here before the king's meeting.

"Father Aiken?"

It seems Hilla had been attempting to gain my attention.

"Lady Aedre has asked to speak with me in private. She will escort me back to my chamber."

The lady was not asking, but if she had been, I would not have encouraged such a meeting. The two women had spoken throughout the meal, and by the looks Lady Aedre had been giving Hilla, my guess is that she senses something. Or perhaps her husband said more than he should have.

Either way, I like it not.

But she is no longer my captive. And is nothing to me, really, but a woman who, after tomorrow, I will likely never see again. King Galfrid has secured her passage to Breywood in two days' time.

I stand and take Hilla's hand in mine as she rises. Ignoring the jolt of awareness that passes between us, I return to my seat and watch as the two women walk away. Straining to hear their words, a different type of awareness makes the hairs on my neck stand as I read Lady Aedre's lips.

"You have been chosen."

22

HILLA

"Chosen?"

Following the very beautiful Lady Aedre from the hall, my instinct that she is a friend and not foe, we walk through corridors lit only by torches that line the walls, until we come to a closed door.

"Our own quarters are so far away, but this will suffice." She opens the door.

I gasp at the colors inside. "Tis a miniature version of the great hall."

Tapestries line the walls, the candlelight in Lady Aedre's hand the only source of light until she moves from table to table, at least four of which she's reached already, lighting candles on each one.

"Tis called the small hall. Used by the Curia when they are not meeting with the king."

That the lady is able to come into this chamber, even given her husband's position, says much about her status here at court.

"Come," she says. "Sit. We have much to discuss."

I do sit then, the velvet-cushioned high-back chair scraping the stone flooring.

"I apologize for all the mystery surrounding my request," she begins. "And for the requests I am about to make."

I stare blankly at the woman, who reaches out her hands, palms facing upward.

"Will you give me your hands, Lady Hilla?" Before I can say yea or nay, she adds, "I am a Garra."

I'm unable to hold back my surprise at the revelation.

A Garra.

So few of them remain on the Isle, and even fewer who practice openly. My mother had a special affinity for the women healers, and their teachings, but even so I've met only one in my entire life.

"A Garra," I repeat. Unlike most healers, the Garra specialize in matters of the heart and all those afflictions and blessings that arise from it. From love to childbirth, they are also said to harness special powers that, to some, seem unnatural. To others, miraculous. "I did not know."

"Of course you did not," she says as I give the woman my hands. Though I've known her for only one evening, it feels as though Lady Aedre and I are better acquainted. Silly, but true nonetheless.

Lady Aedre's fingers wrap around mine as she closes her eyes. I watch her, thinking of the words she said on the way from the hall. Thinking of Aiken's expression when I said I was leaving with her, as if he was concerned for my safety.

Thinking of what had nearly happened in my chamber.

Markedly absent from my thoughts . . . my husband's death.

"Tis as I thought." She releases my hands, pulls her own back and continues to stare. "Remarkable."

"Do you . . . can you see things?" I am unsure, precisely, what the Garra's capabilities are. None seem to know much aside from the certainty that they are exceptional healers. And that their ancestor's blood must run through them in order to be considered Garra and not simply a skilled healer.

"Not precisely. Tis a feeling, is all. Most often, a fleeting one that I do not understand. But you . . ." She blinks. "I've a friend back home, in Murwood End. His name is Kipp Aldwine. You are somehow connected to him. And you bring hope." She frowns. "When we supped, I was overcome by this feeling of contentment in your presence. As if . . . as if all would be well. A feeling that you had been chosen. I believe my instinct was correct."

None of this makes sense to me.

"Chosen? For what?"

She shakes her head. "That I do not know."

"I believe," I say, thinking aloud, "perhaps you sense my sister in me. The queen. She is the chosen one of Edingham and will bring peace to this isle."

I say it with so much confidence I surprise even myself. Tis an odd notion, to be sure. We are on the verge of war as certain as we were before the Battle of Hendrelds Hill. I'd been just a child then, but I can easily remember the same tensions that ran high between our kingdoms. As they do now.

"Nay," Lady Aedre says, her voice firm. "Tis not your sister but you. I must think on this."

She stands and begins to pace, her cream gown swishing around her feet. "I could ask my husband," she says to herself, "but if he does not agree . . ."

I watch in fascination, interrupting just once.

"Lady Aedre?"

"Aedre," she says, spinning toward me.

She is forthright, this Voyager. But I very much enjoy it.

"Hilla," I offer in return, forgetting my original question.

"Listen carefully, Hilla," she says finally, sitting next to me once again. "I will tell you something very important. But first, I would have your word not to share the information with any other."

Looking into her eyes, I trust her more than I should. More than my father would think prudent. And perhaps even Cettina too. But I am not my sister, and so I must forge my own path, now as a widow. As a woman, for the first time in many, many years, who is free.

"Tell me, and I shall give it," I say without the caution that should hold me back. I'm no Garra, for certain, but something about Aedre speaks to me.

"You must give me your word that you'll not return immediately to Edingham. I know not how you will be needed here. Or what role you shall play. Only that you will be important in the days to come."

She could have asked for anything else, and I might have done it. But to not return to my sister? She needs my counsel. I need to speak to her about my future. About all that occurs here, in Meria. So much must be done.

"Aedre—"

"I would not ask if it were unnecessary. Please, believe me as your mother would have done."

My back straightens.

"Rumors of your mother's reverence for my kind followed her for many years," she says. "I met the queen once, many years ago. She traveled north to Murwood to pay respects when my mother passed away. My grandmother spoke highly of her, and the Garra, in turn, told us tales of your family. Of your mother, and even of you and your sister."

"I am sorry for your mother," I tell her, the connection between us strengthening.

"My grandmother has since passed as well. There are so few of us remaining. Please," Aedre pleads. "Please vow this to me. I can guarantee your safety here at court. My husband will protect you."

As will Aiken, while he remains. Which will not be for much longer. The thought has plagued me since we arrived.

"I believe it to be so. But . . ." How do I tell her without explaining what I've been through these past years? "My husband, he is dead."

Aedre crosses herself. "To the devil he should go. He mistreated you, and his kingdom."

My jaw drops open. How does she know this?

"Vow to me," she repeats again. And though I want nothing more than to return to Cettina, I also know I'll not deny this woman, one I just met. She is Garra. And I am a woman who believes in other women.

Tis enough.

"You have my vow," I say, my voice low but firm.

Aedre grabs my hands once again. Though this time, her eyes remain open. "Then I have much to explain to you. We will start with your travel companion."

My heart skips a beat.

"Father Aiken?"

Aedre shakes her head.

"Nay, tis simply Aiken. The man is a warrior, aye. And a powerful one, like the Shadow Warriors he calls brothers. But he is no Elderman."

23

AIKEN

"*K*ind of you to seek me out on your return."

Father Silvester attempts to intimidate me as he does all others. But I do not flinch nor look away. When I first joined the order, I was warned my insolence would see me punished, but that never came to pass.

Tall, thin, and incredibly resourceful, the man has barely seen fifty summers, and yet, he controls more of the Isle than anyone realizes. The church's rising influence under his leadership has mostly to do with Silvester's relentless pursuit of more coin and power.

No one knows better than I how far he is willing to go for both.

"Forgive me," I say, falling into step with the Prima as he walks away from the throne room. The moment I learned he'd arrived at court this morn to meet with the king, I sought him out but missed him before he'd gone inside. His personal guards, men whose moral code equals the Prima's own quite questionable one, watch with justified suspicion.

I was recruited for my skill and willingness to take the Elderman's vow, but not being a religious man myself, I have never forged a relationship with any of the others. Good men, their deeds pure, were overshadowed by the Prima's greed. The longer I serve him, the more I think his presence will not bode well for the future of the church.

"I was carrying out your wishes, Father."

Instead of responding, he walks faster.

I don't need to ask about his meeting. After speaking with the king myself, and given Silvester's demeanor now, I already know its outcome.

"I would speak with you privately, Father."

Although he is angry now, my proposal should put him at ease. But instead of answering, he continues toward the great hall, and past it, confirming my suspicions. If he and King Galfrid had somehow worked out an accord, he would be remaining for the midday meal.

It is only as we reach a fairly empty, long corridor that Silvester stops and waves away the two guards trailing us. Shadow Warriors, men whose skill surprised me when I first joined them, fade into the background as Silvester berates me with his eyes.

"You've been in the capital for three days."

"Aye, Father. Doing the work you set before me."

Clearly he does not wish to speak openly here. Trying the closest door to us, not expecting it to be open, I am surprised when the latch gives. And immediately nod for the Prima to enter.

He does so, reluctantly, as I shut the door behind us. A small solar of some type, empty, serves my purposes well.

"I've much to tell you, Father."

He trusts me, oddly. Even as he wishes it were otherwise.

"We go to war, Aiken. The Highlanders are no longer my concern."

For an intelligent man who has amassed more wealth and property for the church during his ten years of leadership than any time before him, the Prima can be extraordinarily shortsighted. His failure to see that Edingham's fate is tied to that of Meria is a blind spot I will gladly take advantage of.

"You know I travel with the queen's sister?" I ask him, aware he will be apprised of all that has transpired since I returned to d'Almerita.

"Aye, and you will explain how such a thing came about."

Prepared to launch into the story I've set in my head, Silvester cuts me off.

"But not here. We must get back to Avalon immediately."

We go to war.

"You will side with Hinton and oppose the king?"

The stubborn set of his jaw confirms it. I would tell him doing so was a mistake. Would attempt to convince him otherwise. But I am not that far in Silvester's good graces. He only tells me anything of consequence because I'm willing to overlook his questionable judgment and carry out his bidding, and because of my skill with the sword.

So it is done. As Galfrid predicted.

This came as little surprise after all the revelations the day before, including the news that still had me reeling when I woke this morn—that Silvester was only here to try to blackmail the king. Even I underestimated the Prima's ambitions.

Apparently Lord Hinton promised Silvester a seat in his Curia, something Galfrid would never agree to. And now that the king had denied Silvester, apparently he would openly support the nephew's claim. No small matter. Between Silvester's coin, and his warriors, it could mean the difference between victory and defeat.

"We will do what is necessary for the church," he snaps.

"Of course," I agree immediately. "And I will come with you, if that is your will. You should know, however, for my role in returning the princess safely, I've gained a measure of trust from the king."

Silvester scoffs at the notion. "What does he care for Edingham's princess?"

Treading carefully, I attempt to explain. "As you know, the attack at Craighcebor did not go as planned. Whitley was captured." I offer information he does not have access to yet to gain his trust. "And executed."

His surprise is evident.

"Executed? How did you come by such news?"

I ignore the question. "The king has been mollified by Queen Cettina's swift punishment. When her sister returns, unharmed—"

"It will be another step toward peace between them," he finishes. "Even so, the queen will not involve herself in Merian politics. She will not forgive the king after what he's done."

Only through instability does Silvester attain his goals. So I offer an incentive for the opposite.

"The princess has done much to ensure improved relations between her country and Meria."

He scoffs at that. "She's been here mere days."

True enough, and I've not seen Hilla since she left the meal with Aedre. This morn I tried to find her but was told she'd already left her chambers. "Even so, a bond between her and the king has been formed," I lie.

Silvester's shoulders rise and fall, his birdlike eyes narrowed. "Out with it," he demands, impatient.

We agreed this could be a dangerous strategy. But a boldness that will buy Galfrid some time is needed.

"This morn I was privy to a conversation and learned the king sends a party north, to Murwood End. An odd move given the circumstances, do you not agree?"

Silvester appears thoughtful. "Exceedingly odd," he agrees.

"I can offer my services. To accompany them, pray for safe passage. And find out why he sends these men to Murwood End." The implication, that Galfrid does so to garner their support in the upcoming war. But nothing could be further from the truth.

Silvester watches me closely. If he denies my request and takes the information beyond this chamber, we can only hope he does not discover the truth. The Prima believes he's backing the man who will be the next king of Meria. Indeed, Lord Hinton may have the support of those who blame Galfrid for the disaster that was the Oryan. For allowing his only son and heir to drown along with two hundred of Meria's best warriors, as if the king would have wished for such a thing to occur.

He clearly believes Hinton will prevail, and now that Galfrid has refused to be blackmailed, Silvester seems content to cut ties with one of the greatest kings this Isle has ever seen. What he does not know is that Galfrid's bastard son lives. And though his Voyager son has refused to take his rightful place as heir, one final attempt at convincing him to do so might be my greatest mission ever.

Although I would do it as an Elderman, if possible. If the mission fails, if war does come to Meria, I would at least still be positioned to aid the king as Silvester's man.

"We will need your skill when the fighting begins," he said.

He will do it. I try not to let my relief show.

"They would sail forthwith. It will take weeks for Hinton to get into position, and I will have returned by then."

Silvester looks at the door, aware he remains inside the castle of a man he essentially just declared war against.

"Do it," he says. "But this time, when you return, I'll expect more than vague notions

Or: I'll have more than vague notions of your exploits, lest I begin to question your loyalty, Father Aiken."

"Of course." I bow in deference to a man I hate. "I will not fail you."

"You do the work of the church. Remember that."

As he leaves, I school my expression into indifference as his guards saunter past. Once alone, finally, I let out a breath.

The first move has just been made. The game, begun.

The stakes? The future of Meria.

"You are well prepared, Princess."

"Lady," I correct the maid, realizing Meria has not had a princess in some time. "Although I am a princess, I am simply Lady Hilla," I explain.

"Lady Hilla. You do look beautiful this eve."

Indeed. Another day, another gown. This one even lovelier than the first. In my conversation with the king, I'd been completely remiss in thanking him for the first one.

"Many thanks, mistress."

"Shall I fetch you an escort?"

Even as she speaks, I follow her to the door. "I do believe I know the way to the hall. But I thank you for your kindness."

As the maid turns right, I make my way left, down the whitewashed corridor, lit with wall torches. And quickly regret declining her offer. Castle d'Almerita is a maze unlike any castle I've been in before.

Spying a servant at the end of the corridor, I am about to ask the way to the hall when a sound to my left beckons. I follow it, marveling that the air is still warm even though I am now outside. I look down and gasp.

Although I knew Castle d'Almerita was built on a cliff, I've not yet had the opportunity to see its southernmost side. The view is simply breathtaking. Just below, light from torches all along the walls and moonlight from above illuminate the sea below. The bustle inside is so different from the quiet peace that can be found here. As waves crash against the rock wall beneath me, I am too mesmerized to move. Some say Meria was bewitched by the original Garra who broke the Isle. I say, seeing this, it is merely blessed. Besides, she did not break the Isle into two. Aye, Lady Edina received a love potion that made King Onry fall in love with her, setting the course for their son to leave, but a long series of choices are to blame for the rift, not a single action. As an Easterner, I've a great respect for those who fought to make Edingham the kingdom it is today.

But nay, I do not believe Meria is cursed.

"Hilla?"

How did he find me here?

I am not ready to speak to him. In fact, I will likely never be ready. I watch as Aiken steps onto the stone walkway. Wearing his robes, Aiken appears every bit the Elderman he poses as.

I have so many questions after Aedre's revelations. She could not say, precisely, why he posed as an Elderman, but only that she'd overheard enough of her husband's conversations the past few days to know Aiken was allied with the king and that he spied on Father Silvester. And, of course, that I would be instrumental in bringing peace to the Isle, though she could not say precisely how. We'd talked well into the night. Of Meria. Of Edingham. And Murwood End. Sharing tales of our childhood and dreams for the future of the Isle.

I admitted that it was my sister's fervent hope to cease the terrible animosity between two neighbors that will forever be bound by a shared past, and by a border that stretches nearly the entire Isle. We spoke of arranged marriages, of my father's descent into darkness, and of my hope for the future.

I thanked her for sharing her knowledge of Aiken with me, to which she responded, "I would not break a confidence of my husband's, but since he did not directly tell me of Aiken's deception, and since I am convinced you will play a vital role in all of this, it felt as if it was my duty to tell you."

Together, we forged a path forward. One Cettina would welcome. Of that, I am sure.

"Aiken," I greet him.

I'd been extremely angry at first. But this morn, when I woke, I thought of how little anger served my father. Of how, for the first time in years, I have no master. A widow, afforded more freedom than most women, and a princess no longer exiled.

Nay, tis the time for hope, not anger. Even still, I'd not sought him out, unsure what to say.

"A servant saw you coming this way. You are a difficult woman to find."

He looks out, breathing deeply. And is as affected as I'd been when I first ventured out here.

"Of all the places on the Isle, this is undoubtedly the most beautiful."

"I've heard," I venture, "the Cliffs of Murh in Murwood End have that distinction."

"They are striking, to be sure. But always so cold." Continuing to look out to the sea, he says, "I am leaving on the morrow."

I realize then, Aiken is sad. A rare emotion from my companion, which I've only glimpsed when he speaks of his mother's unwillingness to come to Meria. Apparently he's asked her many, many times. Has offered her housing, and protection, and work, if she so desires. I'd wondered how an Elderman had enough coin to do such a thing.

"Aye?" I respond.

Frowning, he gives me the same look that I once mistook for longing, having believed it could not be so. But I do not mistake his look now. It is longing. Desire. How could I have doubted it before?

"You should not fear for your safety here," he says. "You will be escorted to the port by the king's own guards. Finally reunited with your sister."

"Where will you go?" I ask, knowing the answer already.

Aedre came to my chamber earlier and told me Aiken had convinced Father Silvester of his need to accompany the king's retinue north, to Murwood End. But that had not been her biggest revelation. I could not have predicted what she next revealed.

The king has another son, born out of wedlock. A man living in Murwood End whom Galfrid would attempt to convince one last time to come south, to take his place as the king's heir.

At first Aedre's husband had been mortified, she admitted, that Aedre had told me of the king's secret. So few knew of it, and yet Aedre shared the knowledge with his king's enemy. Aedre reminded her husband that Kipp Aldwine was her dearest childhood friend, and if anyone had the right to reveal his secret, 'twas her.

Besides, she had argued, I was not the enemy he believed me to be. Aedre told him of our discussion of peace, of my sister's desire to end the feuding. So it had been decided that I would accompany the king's men, including Aiken, north. It was where Aedre sensed I belonged.

So nay, this was not goodbye. But I'd begged Aedre to allow Aiken to keep his secrets from me. If he wanted to tell me he was not an Elderman, then he would do so. In his time.

It seemed, in theory, a good plan. But now, standing before him, I do not know how long this deception between us can last.

"I will continue to serve my master," he says, and I realize he does not mean Silvester. Thus, Aiken does not lie. On this matter, at least.

So many partial truths between us.

"I will miss you, Aiken," I say softly. Not tomorrow, but after the journey north is ended.

For a moment, I think he means to kiss me. This time, I would return it. Welcome it. Feel no guilt for it.

Instead, he reaches his hand to pull a strand of hair into his fingers.

"I woke one morn," he says, "with my hand entangled in your hair. I must have reached out in the night without realizing it."

"The same morn as the one we spied the farmer and his son on the road?"

He continues to thread my hair through his fingers.

"You were awake?"

"Aye."

I am no longer a married woman. Aiken, never a man of God. And yet, his honor prevents him from leaning forward.

So I do it instead.

I close the gap between us and tilt my head up to him. In response, Aiken freezes, watching me.

Parting my lips, I stand on my tiptoes. And leave nothing to fate. Reaching for his shoulders and clutching the material of his robes, I pull him down to me.

Aiken's grasp on my hair loosens, only to slide to the back of my head. Thankfully, my husband never kissed me. Not once in all those years. Kissing 'twas not necessary to conceive a child, and I'd been grateful for it.

But Aiken clearly thinks I know how to proceed, and I do not.

"Open your mouth for me, Hilla," he demands.

So I do.

Aiken's tongue sweeps inside, and I touch my own to his. Weeks of exchanged glances, of accidental—and not so accidental—touches, all ignite at this very moment. His lips coax my own to explore, and I gladly accept the invitation.

Vaguely I hear the waves crash against the cliffs below as I'm drawn deeper and deeper into him. With every passing moment, my body of its own accord melds closer to his. We're bound together, and no part of me wishes it otherwise.

When he groans against my lips, I do the same.

When he presses the back of my head even closer, I wrap my hands around him.

When he tilts his head for better access, I give it.

Unapologetically.

"Hilla," he gasps, stepping back so quickly it takes a moment for me to realize the kiss has ended. "Hilla," he repeats, looking at me. Stricken. Full of an emotion I cannot name. "I'm so sorry."

As if it were he that kissed me.

"I'm sorry. Hilla. For everything."

With that, he pivots and strides back the way he came.

I touch my fingers to my lips. Had I known . . . had I known it could be that way, I'd have mourned for the loss of passion, of love, long ago.

Thankful for the first time for my ignorance of what is possible between a man and a woman, I close my eyes, remembering. It happened just a moment ago, that kiss. And yet already it feels a lifetime since Aiken pressed his lips to mine.

Now that I know what it is to be well and truly kissed.

"*F*ather Aiken!" The king's commander waves from across the courtyard. I wait for him, ready to begin my journey. After last eve, I'm thankful for the mission. Anything to force me away from her.

She is no longer a married woman, aye. But I am an Elderman, of sorts, the only spy remaining in Silvester's employ. If Hinton attempts to force Galfrid's hand, an increasingly likely scenario, the Prima's power will only grow. Left unchecked, I've no doubt the Isle will be worse off for it.

Not once since the day Baldric found me, trained me, gave me a purpose, have I betrayed him or the Legion. Left here, with Hilla, I fear for my own actions. No woman has inflamed me, touched my soul, like this one.

"A word before you depart?"

"Good day," I say to the commander as he approaches. I shake his hand.

"I'd have spoken to you last eve," he says, "but you did not attend the meal."

"My regrets," I say, not regretting my absence at all, given my will to keep myself from Hilla has been all but broken since the news of Whitley's death. "The men await," I remind him, the others emerging one by one from the stables across the courtyard.

He advances toward me, darting wary glances left and right. There is naught unusual about the king's commander speaking to an Elderman. But clearly he does not wish to be overheard.

"There has been a . . . development since we last spoke."

"A development?"

"Aye, my wife. As you know, she is Garra," he says, and I nod in acknowledgment. "She had a vision, of sorts."

A vision. Few Garra have this ability.

"Aedre does not know when or how the princess will aid our cause. Or even why, as her fate would not seem to intertwine with our present affairs in Meria."

The princess.

I think back to the first night we arrived, when Lady Aedre left with Hilla. Searching his eyes for answers, I see the commander's concern for the first time.

And then I see her.

Striding toward us, wearing a gown I've not seen before, one suited for travel, Hilla's eyes find mine.

No. She cannot.

"Lady Hilla has agreed to travel to Murwood End with you."

"Agreed to travel?" I turn my attention back to the commander. "She is leaving for Edingham, to return to her sister. Why would she come north with us?"

The commander lowers his voice even more as Hilla approaches. "We do not know. But Aedre wills it, and the princess has agreed. She and my wife have developed a bond these past days."

A bond. Dear God, no.

"She is Garra," he repeats, knowing what I am. My hesitation has naught to do with Lady Aedre. I do not question her vision but the situation itself. I cannot do this.

"You do not understand," I start as the lady in question finds us.

D'Abella smiles knowingly. "Aye, I think I do. And trust you will find a way to navigate it."

He knows of my desire for her.

"Another vision?" I ask wryly.

"Nay," he says to me. "The simple use of my eyes." The commander then turns to Hilla to greet her.

"Good day, Lord d'Abella. Father Aiken."

This cannot be.

"Lady Hilla."

She knew last eve. I cannot wait to speak to Hilla alone. How could she have stood there and not told me? She allowed me to believe it was the last we would see each other.

There's much you do not share with her.

But this is different.

"I trust Lord d'Abella apprised you of my accompaniment? It seems as if the others are prepared to leave for the docks, aye?"

I say nothing, but she knows full well we will be having a discussion, alone. Soon.

It was agreed that I would seek out Aldwine and inform him of the Prima's involvement and plans to extend his influence into the north. None believed it would alter his stance, but with Hinton's growing support, and the dissolution of Silvester's alliance with the king, Galfrid's victory is less certain, and we have no choice but to try once again to convince Aldwine to take his rightful place. Lord d'Abella will not be joining the expedition north, however, as Galfrid's commanders are needed here. Instead, d'Abella's man Salvi was chosen to accompany me. He too would seek an audience with Aldwine, but under different circumstances. Salvi is to serve as the king's representative. I am to carry a message from Lady Aedre.

"Aye," d'Abella answers for me. "You best be off. May your journey be safe, your trade, a success."

Avoiding Hilla, I nod to the commander. We fully expect when next we meet Meria will be engaged in an internal battle for its future. This will be but one final effort to chart a new course. And it seems, for me, a test of the vow I did take.

2 6

HILLA

*A*lthough not my first sea journey, this is certainly a different sort of ship than I traveled on as a princess of Edingham. Grateful for a private cabin, as I'm told only the captain and myself have such, I sit on the bed. A small desk, dressing table and shelves, along with my own chest, are my only companions for nearly a fortnight.

It has been a long day.

Every so often, I would catch Aiken watching me. He's said nothing since this morn, the tension between us not going unnoticed by the crew. The day was not wholly unpleasant, however. After spending the afternoon on deck marveling at the high whistle of the wind and the deep curves of the sail's' leeches, I accepted an offer by the captain to dine with him. A kind man, his hair mostly white and his voice as deep as I imagine the sea water beneath us to be, he asked many questions about Edingham. This route, from d'Almerita to Murwood End, and sometimes even north of Murwood to Midenear, is the only one he travels. He indicated it has been many years since he's stepped foot on the shores of Edingham.

Aiken must have eaten with the other men. And although enough sunlight would likely make for a spectacular view above deck, the strain of being around him, and not speaking, has driven me here, below decks. Being down here, to avoid the strain, has put me in a foul mood, making it increasingly difficult to remember that kiss. Too easy to dwell on his deception.

I grab a wooden post as the ship jolts. I've not become accustomed to such sudden movements yet, although the captain assures me I will, likely just in time to disembark. I consider removing my boots but decide, if the waters remain calm, to go back on deck to see the night sky without hindrance.

I just need a moment to think. To reflect. Perhaps I should have told him last eve. Deciding not to be angry with his deception and actually being so were not one and the same. Some of my irritation with him remains, even as I know it serves no purpose.

I nearly fall from the bed at the quick succession of knocks at the door. I stand, opening it, not surprised to see Aiken standing there in his Elderman robes.

"Lady Hilla."

He fills the frame, this man that so struck fear in his adversaries they would turn coward and run rather than engage with him. For my purposes, I cannot look at him without remembering that kiss. My anger gives way to desire, as it does so often with him.

"I would speak to you."

"Will the others not think it strange?"

"Do you care what the others think?"

Stepping aside, acknowledging that I do not, I close the door behind him. Aiken fills the small cabin as he did the doorframe, so I ask for him to sit.

Aiken moves to the sole chair nailed to the floorboard

below. I sit on the edge of the bed just in time. There's another jolt of the ship, this one stronger than the last.

How he knew what I was feeling, I'm not sure. I've never met a man as astute as Aiken.

I think back to the day we met. "That is untrue."

"That first day, perhaps. But even after you knew what I was, you fought me at every turn."

I rein in my instinct to tell Aiken I've no notion of what, or who, he really is.

"What of 'I will miss you,' Hilla?"

He repeats my words from last eve back to me. Aiken is still angry.

"I will miss you." I raise my chin, defiant. "When we do part. And you may scowl if you like, Aiken. But until you can say you keep no secrets from me, your anger is misplaced."

My words hit their mark. His features soften, if just a bit.

"Why did you not tell me you were traveling to Murwood End?" he asks.

"I might ask the same."

His eye twitches.

I take a deep breath. "Why did you not tell me you are no Elderman?"

Aiken goes completely still.

He stares at me, and I stare back. We do not break eye contact for a long time, the swaying movements of the ship oddly comforting.

"Who told you?"

"Lady Aedre."

"She had no right."

"As you have no right to chastise me for keeping secrets. *Father* Aiken."

He shoots up from the chair, closing the space between us so quickly I react by standing as well.

"You knew last eve."

"Aye."

His chest heaves in anger. And maybe something else.

"What did she tell you?"

We stand so close, the cabin both confining and warm, though not overly so.

"She told me you are no Elderman. That you aid the king, though she does not know why. That she had a vision, that I would play an important role in Murwood End. Lady Aedre convinced me to make the journey here rather than back to Breywood."

His jaw set, Aiken says nothing.

"And then I understood," I say, bolder than I'd intended.

"What did you understand?"

Although Aiken doesn't move, I know well how this will end.

"I understood how a man who pledged himself to God could look at me the way you did throughout our journey to the south."

"If you understand at all, you'll not provoke me, Hilla."

Nay, Aiken is wrong. I've lived for my sister these past years. But this night is for me.

"Provoke you?" I pretend to misunderstand, closing the distance between us. "I do nothing save answer your questions. More than you've ever done with me."

His lips part.

"What is holding you back, Aiken?"

His shoulders heave with the effort of restraint.

"'Tis I who is a widow of mere days. Who learned the man who captured her only posed as an Elderman. And yet you stand before me hesitant. Even though I know you want to kiss me."

With every bold word that comes from my mouth, my shoulders pull back. My chin rises. I will not be held down any longer.

"I want to do more than kiss you, Hilla. *That* is what holds me back."

If it is a sin to want to be with a man so soon after becoming a widow, then God may count me a sinner.

"I want more too, Aiken."

There are so many reasons this is a bad idea. The fact that her traitorous husband was just recently killed is not among them. But I can think of plenty of others.

But there's also one good reason to pull Hilla into my arms.

And so, I do.

This time, tis not a kiss meant to deceive. Or one born out of desperation at the thought of never seeing her again. This kiss is one of pure desire. Of respect. Of reverence, even. Our tongues tangle, my hands wasting no time untying the laces of her overcoat, which I've been eyeing since she stepped on this ship. Because I've imagined my fingers doing this very thing, the ties come loose rather easily.

I press my lips harder, coaxing Hilla's tongue into a rhythm neither of us will be able to stop. With every sweep, her gown loosens. Loath to pull away from her, but glad now I've done so as it affords my eyes a feast, I watch as Hilla assists me until she wears nothing but a shift and hose.

"I would make love to you, Hilla," I tell her, loosening the leather belt at my waist. "I would bury myself so deep inside you," I say, making quick work of my robes and linen shirt as Hilla stares, "as I've wanted to do from that first day."

Hilla's lips part as I rid myself of my boots after tossing my shirt on her bed. Now standing before her in nothing but breeches, I wait for her permission. And think to reassure her.

"I will not get you with child," I promise, the muscles in my buttocks clenching at the thought of pulling out once inside her. How many nights did I lie beside Hilla thinking of this? Too many, and nothing but her words will stop it.

"You can assure such a thing?"

I pull her toward me again.

"Aye."

With just a thin slip of material between us, her breasts pressing against my chest, I await her response by allowing my hands to roam.

And roam they do.

Down to the hem of her shift, where I grab the material in anticipation.

"I would make love to a man who does not despise me. One who treats me kindly."

Her admission reminds me that, even if she's not been physically abused, she has been so in every other way. Pulling upward, slowly with anticipation, I make a vow to her.

"I will revere you as you deserve, Hilla."

Tis good the words have already left my mouth. Now that Hilla is completely nude, I'd not have been able to speak. Light from the sole lantern in her small cabin illuminates every curve. Grabbing her hands, I place them on my chest.

"The night I was in the tub," I tell her, my thumbs reaching out and circling both nipples. "I saw you watching me."

Finally, hesitantly at first, she begins her own exploration.

The featherlight touch of her fingertips on my chest makes me wonder how long this could possibly last.

Go slowly with her, Aiken. She is a virgin in the ways that matter most.

"If you knew how badly I wanted to do this," I say as my hand lowers, finally cupping her. "And this."

Her expression when I slip inside tells me all I need to know of the bastard she'd been married to. Hilla's hands freeze on my chest, her eyes wide. But I do not relent. Pushing inside, gliding and circling, I silently give thanks to my early instructors in this dance of desire.

"Aiken," she breathes, "I did not know."

I press first my palm, and then my body, against her, as closely as I'm able with my arm between us. Kissing her, I show Hilla all that is possible between a man and a woman that has naught to do with producing an heir.

Bringing her pleasure is my only goal now, even as the ship lurches beneath us. The men will know I'm in her cabin, though all but Hilla and Salvi believe me to be an Elderman.

"Aiken," she cries against my mouth. Alarmed, I pull away. Or try to. But she grabs my hand, staying it. Which is when I realize what is happening. If Whitley weren't dead already, I would kill the man myself.

"Tis normal," I say, watching her face as I guide her toward the bed. Pulling my hand away, I tell her what to expect. Something, I suspect, none have done before. Not even before she was married.

But then who would have done so? Her mother had died, her sister, the queen, younger than she and inexperienced. Was there not even a maid to do so?

Making quick work of my breeches, and realizing I've done nothing to allay her fears as she stares at me now, I talk quickly.

"You've not made love, Hilla. I intend to rectify that.

Those feelings, when my fingers were inside you . . . you will feel so again. Despite what many will say, the pleasure that derives from this . . ." I kneel between her legs, grateful there is no bunk above us; the bed is small, but large enough to accommodate us. ". . . is not something to be ashamed of. Nor to shy away from. And aye," I answer as she opens her mouth to speak, "I am an expert on such matters."

Hilla laughs.

"From having done this so often?" she teases.

"Mmm." I spread her legs and lower myself, until Hilla realizes what I intend.

"Aiken! Certainly you cannot . . ."

If Hilla is to have her first climax, it will be with my tongue against her. So ignoring her indignation, I spread my lovely princess even wider. And proceed to show her how wrong she is.

I can. And I will.

No sooner does my tongue begin to coax her into the climax she nearly had before we stopped than Hilla's hands are wound through my hair. Tasting her, loving her with my mouth, I am unsurprised she quickly releases, her legs trembling around me as I smile against her in sweet victory.

"Nay, Hilla. You forget from whence I came."

Eyes wide, she watches, still panting, as I position myself above her.

"You know now," I say, guiding myself closer, "I am no Elderman. Nor could I ever be so, for the thought of doing this"—I slowly push inside, Hilla still so very wet—"has consumed nearly every waking moment of mine since we met."

Hilla, barely recovered, grips my shoulders.

"Had I known," she says, "it would have consumed mine too."

Laughing, and at the time burying myself fully inside her, I close my eyes. Seeing her, being joined this way . . .

"You are in pain," she says, obviously concerned.

My eyes shoot open as I begin to move.

"I've been in pain since the day you wriggled this"—I slip my hand under her buttocks, squeezing—"against me when we rode away from Craighcebor."

"I did no such thing."

Taking advantage of my hand's position, I use it to pull us closer.

"Mayhap not intentionally, Hilla, but I can assure you." I circle my hips as I hold myself atop her. "You did."

I could so easily come inside her, but I won't. Not now. Not ever. But I will show her how it should be between a man and a woman.

"I would kiss you, but then I couldn't see your face," I say as Hilla's expression changes from sheer wonder to pleasure as we move. Thrusting with increasing speed, I'm not so untrained to believe she will climax this way alone. As I dip my hand between us once again, Hilla's hips push upward more urgently.

"This is not . . . that is to say, I know some enjoy this but —" She stops. No words are needed.

"This," I assure her, "is as it should be."

When Hilla's lips part and her thighs begin to quiver, I do not relent. When her nails dig into my shoulders, I relish the sensation.

"Aiken . . ."

Ah God, if I thought riding beside her and lying so close to her were difficult, not giving myself over completely to Hilla at this moment is much more so. Burying myself inside her, my arms shaking with the effort, I'm rewarded by a cry of pleasure likely to be heard by all on the ship.

As she clenches around me, I keep my promise and pull

out, grabbing my shirt just in time. As discreetly as possible, I remove myself from her reluctantly. With little time to relish my own release, I attempt to conceal the evidence of my need for Hilla.

But she sees me.

Blissfully spent, but curious, Hilla watches as I drop my shirt on the ground.

"To ensure you will not beget a child from this," I explain. But still, she looks at me. Gathering Hilla in my arms as I lie next to her in the small bed, I push her hair from my face, back over her shoulder.

"Does it . . . does it feel the same for you? Doing that?"

Not meaning to laugh but unable to help it, I tilt Hilla's chin up toward me, kissing her rather than answering. This night was about her pleasure, not mine. Although I enjoyed a fair bit of it as well.

Her lips, so soft and willing, fit with mine more perfectly than they should.

"We can speak on that another time. For now, there are other matters to discuss," I say, finally pulling away.

"Aye," she agrees, "there are."

2 8

HILLA

Two days since our night together, and Aiken and I have yet to find a moment alone. After the captain's knock at my cabin door that eve, we hastily dressed and Aiken smoothed over our private meeting with a story of me worrying about the safety of our voyage.

To maintain the ruse, I've had to pretend, with every lurch of the ship, a fear of being overturned. Feigning weakness is something I became accustomed to as Whitley's wife, when 'twas necessary. But I care less and less to do so. A fact I am determined to share with Aiken, if I could get the man alone.

Unfortunately, a storm has made for a lonely journey in this cramped cabin as Aiken assists the men on deck. Apparently he is a warrior, a monk, and a sailor.

As for my part, soon I will not need to pretend uneasiness on this voyage. All day we rock, from one side to the next. But I tamp down my worry, trust in the skill of the captain, and wait. And think.

Contemplating that night, I wonder what it means. I do

know lovemaking, especially with a widow such as I, can be a very fleeting affair, as Aiken apparently intends for ours to be. Nothing more than simply giving in to a desire.

But was that so bad? Even if short-lived, I will have felt desire like never before.

Other than staying alive, it seems I am incapable of considering anything but each and every touch of Aiken's

Perhaps because I never imagined a love match, not that I am in love with Aiken, of course. But knowing that as the future queen my marriage would be arranged, I spent little time envying those that could pursue their passions. I ignored my maid's attempts to explain the ways between men and women, knowing Whitley was no gentle suitor, and pretended it mattered naught. I did not need a gentle touch but only to ensure my kingdom, now Cettina's kingdom, was safe.

And yet . . .

A knock at the door disrupts my thoughts. As I cross the small space to open it, I notice for the first time the back-and-forth motions that have been ever-present these past two days seem to have ceased.

Pulling open the door, I am surprised to see Aiken standing there. In his Elderman's robes, sword at his side, he is as intimidating as ever. He holds up a jug and two goblets. I glance behind him but see no one.

"The others are occupied."

I step aside, the thudding in my chest that seems to accompany every waking thought of Aiken even stronger now that he's standing next to me. As he comes inside and I close my cabin door, I inadvertently glance at the bed. And imagine him above me.

"The storm has abated?"

If not for him in my cabin, I would desire to venture

above. But now, there is nowhere on this ship I would prefer to be than here.

"Aye."

He puts down the items on the small desk. Before I can say anything more, Aiken pulls me to him, and I willingly meld into his arms. His lips touch mine, differently than that night. They are soft, gentle. Coaxing me, though I need no coaxing at all. Yesterday afternoon he stole inside my cabin for a similar kiss, said nothing, and left. But now, it appears he intends to stay.

"I have thought of little else but that night," he says, pulling away. "If this ship sank, I'd have died a happy man, Hilla." His hands cup my face so gently, tis difficult to imagine he is the same man I traveled with, the one so quick with his sword and so reticent with his words.

"I came to talk," he says, stepping back. "But you are a difficult woman to resist."

"Tis such an odd thing to kiss an Elderman."

The way he looks at me, I know Aiken is thinking about more than kissing.

"I am no Elderman, Hilla. As well you know."

"But you appear as one nevertheless."

He makes a strangled sound, as if walking away from me is painful. Then, pouring two goblets of wine, he hands one to me.

"There are more barrels of Sindridge wine on this ship than passengers," he says, sitting on the small wooden chair. "A fine ship, it did well in the storm."

Taking the goblet to the only other seat, the bed where we made love two nights ago, I sit. And sip. Waiting for I know not what. It seems odd to speak of such mundane things after what we shared. But then, the experience of making love to a man who is not my husband is a new one for me.

Who shall know, precisely, how one should act? Not I, certainly.

"As have you, Hilla."

At first, I do not understand. Until I think on his last words. Aiken knows so little about me, and yet, I can see by the way he looks at me, he truly believes it.

"I've weathered no fewer storms than most." I take a long sip, glad this particular storm is over.

Aiken doesn't answer. Instead, he stands. Removes his belt and sword, then, laying it on the ground next to him, lifts his robes over his head. After draping it across the back of the chair, he sits back down.

"Better?"

In a linen shirt and breeches, he looks like any other nobleman now. Well, perhaps not precisely like just anyone.

"Aye," I admit, realizing I had been staring at his robes. "I've many questions, Aiken."

"Some I cannot answer."

I think of my own secrets and nod.

"How did you come to serve Father Silvester? And in his inner circle, no less." The steady sway of the ship, so much calmer now, is almost comforting.

"I can tell you I came to him an Elderman already. Or supposedly so. My skill with the sword earned me the right to join his personal guard."

"The Shadow Warriors."

"As others call them, aye."

"But you cannot tell me who you serve?" I know the answer before he gives it.

"Nay."

Despite having lain with him, I know Aiken as little now as always. And tell him so. "You've so many secrets."

"As do you, Hilla," he says softly.

He looks directly into my eyes, and though I should not do so, it is my story to tell, so I find my mouth opening. In spite of his secrets, there is no one I trust more, save my sister, than this man. I'd not have given myself to him otherwise.

"Lord Bowes was not a nice man. Nice to look at, perhaps. But he cared little for anyone save himself."

Aiken sits up and leans forward, listening.

"It was neither I nor Cettina who was seen with him in an alcove not far from the great hall. One of my sister's ladies, a woman long jealous of my sister's beauty, was with him that eve. I know not who began the rumor. If it was a servant who saw them together, or the lord or lady themselves, we were never able to discern. But its origins matter little. Once word began to spread, and it became clear Bowes and the lady's maid intended to propagate it, the rumor would not die."

"Rumor that the lady was you?"

I shake my head. "Nay, that it was Cettina."

He appears rightly confused. "I don't understand? How did you . . . ?" Aiken stops. "Dammit, Hilla, you deflected the rumor for your sister," he says, the tic in his jaw revealing his anger. "Why? Why did the couple not simply state the truth? Bowes lost his head for that lie."

"As I said, the lady was jealous of Cettina. As for Bowes, I do not know for certain. Except that he'd tried many times to court my sister. We believe Bowes thought it might force my father to consider him as a suitor." Once the words begin to spill out, ones I've told no one, ever, they do not stop. "Cettina tried to reason with them. Explained that they would both be in grave danger, especially Bowes. But neither would listen."

"Why, Hilla?" His shoulders rise and fall, his eyes flashing. "Why?"

"Cettina was unmarried. She could not endure such a scandal. But I . . ."

"You were married already to Whitley. Better to bear the brunt of his anger, and your father's, than to see Cettina scandalized. But she let you do such a thing?"

I will not let him be angry with my sister.

"She had no choice. I told Father it had been me the servant saw and dared any to deny it."

He downs the rest of his drink and pours another. Light from the small window as the sun begins to set is enough to see clearly. Aiken's eyes fill with unshed tears. His reaction is so unexpected, I forget to continue my story.

"You lost your right to the crown. Endured your husband's wrath. For something you did not do."

His evident pain reminds me of my own. Pain I've long let go, but that resurfaces now as I watch him wrestle with my revelation.

"I never wanted to be queen. Cettina is much better suited to it."

"You have every bit of strength and intelligence as your sister, Hilla."

I begin to deny it, but stop. And think back to these past few weeks. And months. And years.

"I never wanted to be queen," I repeat. "And as for Whitley, I do not believe he'd have been much kinder to me had the affair not happened. He was not a good man."

Aiken is out of his seat so quickly, I do not even have time to stand. He takes the goblet from my hand and places it on the floor, sitting beside me. As he did earlier, Aiken takes my face in his hands.

"You are the bravest, kindest, strongest woman I have ever met, Hilla."

Though his eyes are dry now, mine are not. Before I can stop them, tears slip below my lids and fall onto my face.

Aiken wipes them as they fall, kissing my cheeks. My eyes. And finally, my lips. Desperate for his acceptance, I return his kiss. All the questions I had fall away, unimportant for the moment.

And I can almost believe his words.

29

AIKEN

"Welcome to Murwood End."

The dockmaster greets us as I hold my hand out for Hilla. Galfrid's man watches us. Whether he or the others believe my nightly visits to Hilla were nothing more than discussions, I do not know. There are so many curiosities to this journey, from my very presence to the addition of Lady Hilla, a supposed enemy to Meria—our relationship is just one more.

Not only to the men, but to me as well. I've no notion of what we are doing, spending each night in her cabin, or on deck, talking. Sharing. Laughing.

The ease with which we traveled to Castle d'Almerita continued, despite that second night. We've not spoken of it. And though I've kissed her many times when we were alone, I have not allowed myself to lose control again. My mission as an Elderman in Silvester's personal guard does not include the Princess of Edingham.

And yet . . .

"It has been so many years, and yet, everything looks the same."

Hilla steps onto the dock. The captain shakes Salvi's hand, then the others, as they disembark as well. He will stay with the ship while we are here, though none know how long that might be.

"We will procure lodgings," Salvi says, "at Sailor's Inn. Will you join us there?" he asks, looking from me to Hilla.

"Aye. But I would visit someone first."

"I would accompany you," Hilla says, as I expected.

Salvi nods, seemingly resigned to the fact that Hilla and I will not be separated, even if he must think it odd.

Here in Murwood, even when the sun shines, a cloak is necessary. Hilla pulls hers up around her ears as we leave the crowded docks and head toward the village.

"The king was most kind to provide this. I'd forgotten the chill that pervades even the warmest days up here."

Partially listening to Hilla, and partially noting all of our surroundings—the buildings, the people, anything that could pose a threat—I speak without thinking.

"'Twas not easy to procure."

The bustle of the docks begins to give way as we pass into what is the heart of Murwood End. Its village, though not large by Merian standards, is robust.

It takes a moment for me to realize Hilla has stopped. When I turn to look at her, the princess is staring back at me.

"You sent this to me?"

I blink, realizing only now what I'd said.

"Aye."

A merchant's wagon rolls past us, Hilla moving out of the way only as I reach out to guide her from the center of the dirt street. Behind her, timber-framed two-story buildings with heather-thatched roofs and dead hedges line up one after the other.

"And the gowns?"

"We should move along," I reply, intent on finding the

smith. Aedre bid us to find her father straightaway when we arrived. She assured us he could gain an audience with the king's son. While Salvi and the others would be attempting to do the same, d'Abella and his wife made clear Kipp Aldwine would be unlikely to meet with them. And even less likely to agree to come south with them.

"You had them sent to me?" she asks again.

These past days, I've memorized her every expression. And though Hilla has not asked about my role since that first time, she's wanted to. And that same understandable curiosity is apparent now.

"Each of them, including this"—she tugs on the fur-lined cloak—"must have fetched quite a bit of coin."

"Hilla . . ."

I want to touch her. Kiss her. When we are together, when she is in distress as she was three nights ago when we hit another storm, I'm finding it more and more difficult to hang back. Not to reach out and pull Hilla into my arms at every moment of the day.

"Who are you, Aiken? I do not even know your surname, do you realize that?"

"Furlan," I offer, but she hardly hears me as I'm rushing ahead. "But we must go now to Lorenson."

Another wagon passes us, and Hilla and I move closer to the building nearby, an alehouse from the look of it.

"You are angry I sent you gowns?"

Hilla's brows furrow as she scowls at me. "Nay, Aiken. I am angry that, after all we have been through, you do not tell me who you are truly. That you trust me in all things but with that knowledge."

"I do trust you, Hilla. In all things."

"Except the most important one."

There is nothing I can say, the code more sacred even than what has developed between us. Unless a life hangs in the balance, I cannot, will not, share the one secret she wants me to give.

"Why now?" I ask. "This entire journey you've known, thanks to Lady Aedre, and yet you remained silent. Asking me this as we finally reach Murwood?"

"Because I know you, Aiken. If you wished me to have the knowledge of your identity, you would have told me. But this?" She pats the cloak. "Very few could afford such quality. And tis one of four garments you sent. I do not understand."

Nor will she, ever.

"We must go."

Not waiting for her, I stop a passerby to ask directions to the blacksmith's shop.

"That way, Father. Just to the left of the main gate."

With a quick word of thanks, I breathe in the smell of damp earth with each step, hoping Hilla is behind me. Only after turning a corner, to ensure her safety, do I look back. She is there, still angry, but following me.

After she catches up to me, we walk in silence. The shop comes into view, smoke from its chimney signaling the smithy is indeed inside, and we continue toward it. Entering the building, we find a well-stocked workshop and fine weaponry hanging from poles stretched between the walls. Behind the forge stands a man just as Aedre described him. He looks, for lack of a better description, very much like a blacksmith from Murwood End. It is no wonder he's produced a woman such as Lady Aedre.

Formidable. Like Hilla.

Do not think of her sacrifice now. It would not do anyone well to become angry once again.

Goddamn Bowes. Whitley. Cettina's lady-in-waiting. And worst of all, her father. All but one of them, dead. They should be thankful for it as I'd send all three to their graves again for what they put Hilla through.

"Dal Lorenson?" I ask, pulling down my hood.

"Aye," he says, looking between us.

"I am Father Aiken and this is Lady Hilla, Princess of Edingham."

His surprise is evident.

"We've come with a message from your daughter."

30

HILLA

"This reminds me of Crow's End," I say as we enter the inn. "With more sailors."

"Voyagers," I remind her, the term not always relegated to those who sail and trade from Murwood. Some use it for all those who live in this northern land. One not ruled by either kingdom.

"Do you see them?"

Aiken and I look everywhere, but there is no sign of Salvi or the other men.

"Nay."

He removes his cloak, helps me to do the same, and places them on a metal hanger near the door before nodding to a table in the corner, Aiken's most favorite position. Always separate, away from others. His caution kept me alive, so I should be thankful. Instead, I am becoming increasingly impatient with the reasons for it.

Telling myself that had it not been for Aedre, I'd still think Aiken an Elderman, and that he clearly has no intention to share any more of himself than is necessary, I still am unable to shake the desire to know more.

Dangerously, I've begun to think of a future beyond this mission. Tis difficult to imagine my life without Aiken in it. A silly notion if ever there was one. The man will not even share his true identity with me.

"Two meat pies and ale," he says as we sit, the serving maid curtsying to me.

"Why does she curtsy?" I ask. We were quite clear with Master Lorenson. None should know my true identity.

"Your gown," he says, "marks you as nobility."

"Tis a fine gown," I say, aware of my confrontational tone —I've held back for so many days, it seems I can do so no longer. "But I thought such stations meant little up here, in the north."

"Hilla—"

"My lady. Father," the maid says, placing two mugs of ale on the table. We thank her as she moves away.

Darkness has fallen, and I will admit to being grateful to have Aiken with me. Although there are many similarities between this inn and the others, there is a more ominous air here. I remember being scared as a child of these hardened men with their furs and overly large swords. As an adult, I find myself equally as intimidated as I was then.

Whatever Aiken had been prepared to say when the serving maid came, he no longer seems inclined to do so.

"When do you believe we will gain an audience?" I ask.

The moment I showed the precious gift Lady Aedre had loaned me for this voyage to her father, he had immediately agreed to contact Aldwine. We'd been prepared to tell him everything. From his daughter's strange request for me, a princess of Edingham and no friend to Meria, to accompany Aiken, to the fact that my companion was not truly an Elderman. Instead, he asked no questions. Indeed, he said he needed answers.

Though he had asked after his daughter.

I knew from Aedre that her father followed her to d'Almerita and secured a position as a castle smith. Not long after, he received a missive asking for him to return to Murwood temporarily. His apprentice had fallen ill, leaving none to tend to the forge here. He now trained a new young man to take his place and would then return south.

It afforded him an opportunity, Aedre said, to visit those he missed dearly in Murwood End. Men such as Kipp Aldwine, the only person who could bring a quick end to the war that has likely already seen its first battle in our absence.

Instability in Meria was something I'd have once welcomed. But now, having been too long with a husband who carried only hate in his heart, I feel differently. The Isle is one, even if it was split into two kingdoms many years ago. Cettina believes the same, though she despairs that few Highlanders have the will to help her see unity between us and those from Meria.

"Go with him," Aedre had said. "You are the key, Hilla. If you truly wish to help your sister find peace on this Isle, go."

But her advice did not include anything beyond my presence, my role still unclear to us both. But the excuse to remain with Aiken was strong. And despite our current predicament, despite how much he still holds back from me, I am glad to be here.

With him.

"I do not know. Lorenson seemed to suggest Aldwine could be unpredictable. But at least he is here." He pauses. "If you continue to look at me so . . ."

Aiken doesn't finish. Instead, he watches as two meat pies are placed before us. The maid, as most women seem to do, looks at him with a mixture of appreciation and apprehension. I know the feeling well. A man who looks as he does, but wears the Elderman's robes and the signature sword of the Shadow Warriors . . . part of his appeal, I do believe, is in the combination of such traits.

"You are no longer angry?" he asks when the maid walks away.

"I am." Picking up a spoon, I begin to eat, hungrier than I'd realized. In companionable silence, we finish our meal. Aiken, always watching. Watching me, the hall. Ever vigilant, he misses nothing.

"You are speaking to me, at least."

I push my nearly empty bowl away.

"More than you did when we first met. Tis sometimes difficult to believe you are the same person, Aiken."

I meant it as a jest, a way to lighten the conversation, having tangled with Aiken most of the day. Tis been a long journey. Indeed, a string of long journeys.

"I am prone to more words with you than most."

The admission startles me, although it should not. I've seen him interact with others, and his words ring true. But it hints at an intimacy Aiken seems reluctant to repeat.

"Yet still, you hold back."

"If I had a choice, I would not."

"You always have a choice, Aiken."

Again, we are at an impasse as he says nothing. And so, I change topics.

"Do you believe you, or the men, will be successful in convincing Aldwine?"

Aiken picks up his mug and drinks. "Nay," he says after a long swig. "I do not. If Lady Aedre and d'Abella could not convince him, I've no reason to believe he will change his mind."

"And then?" I ask the question that has lingered over us for days.

"And then, Meria will be at war with itself. Either Galfrid or his nephew will be victorious."

"You say it with such dispassion. As if you do not care about the outcome?"

Aiken frowns. "My thoughts on the matter will not change the circumstances."

I push him further. "Then what will you do?"

Aiken watches me with such intensity, I've nothing to do but drink. I will not squirm in my seat under his gaze. But the longer he watches me, the urge to do so gets stronger.

"That depends," he says finally.

"On?"

Before I can say any more, he sits up straighter in his seat. Knowing him as I do, I find nothing amiss. Salvi is nearly atop us before I see him. How Aiken seems to have eyes others do not, I will never truly understand.

"You are being watched," he says to Aiken, sitting on the stool beside him.

"I am aware."

Watched? By whom?

"We've been unsuccessful thus far," Salvi says, raising his hand to gain the serving maid's attention. "Have you fared any better?"

The maid reaches us, ale in hand. Aiken wraps his fingers around the mug, sliding it to Salvi. Unbidden, the memory of Aiken above me, of how my body responded so easily to him . .. I imagine it happening again.

"We shall see," Aiken says, looking from Salvi to me. Somehow, Aiken seems to know my thoughts. His eyes darken, and then narrow, as if in warning.

Suddenly, the urge to be reckless overtakes me.

"Have you secured rooms?" I ask Salvi, turning away from Aiken.

"Aye, my lady. 'Twas not an easy task. It seems ours was not the only foreign ship to dock today."

"Splendid. I believe I would like a hot bath. Do you think

the innkeeper can arrange it?" I ask innocently. "Slipping into warm water"—I turn to Aiken—"after such a long journey. Does that not sound divine, Father?"

He gives me a look of warning.

"The innkeeper is quite accommodating, for the right amount of coin," Salvi adds. "I believe it could be arranged easily."

"Mmm," I murmur. "A hot bath and a real bed. I do believe I am ready to retire."

In a perfect imitation of the ladies at court who have perfected their flirtations, I smile at Aiken, slowly. With intention. And then address Salvi.

"Would you point me to the innkeeper so I may speak with him?"

Aiken snaps.

"I will do it." He stands up so quickly, Aiken nearly spills his ale.

As he stalks away, I feel no guilt for my performance.

But will he take the bait?

31

AIKEN

I insert the piece of metal into the keyhole, opening her door with ease. She's in the corner of the room, just beside the hearth, both legs propped atop one edge of the wooden tub as she rests inside it. Not surprisingly, Hilla's eyes fly open, her legs dipping back into the water.

"How did you . . . ?"

I hold up the slim piece of metal, closing and locking the door behind me.

"I have the only key," she says, sliding lower into the water.

"Not a key." I toss it onto the floor, along with my belt. And sword. My robes come next.

"Aiken. What are you doing?"

Hair splayed behind her in a curtain of waves, Hilla's hands jut out from the water to grip both ends of the cloth draped across her wooden tub.

"I am undressing," I tell her, aware of the folly of me being here. Of what we are about to do. Again. Forming a deeper attachment to a woman I had so much difficulty leaving in

168

Meria, after all that has happened on the voyage to Murwood
. . .

I should not.

We should not.

And yet, here I am. In her bedchamber. Removing my clothing as quickly as if my life depended on such a deed. She ensured it so belowstairs, in the hall. I'd been resigned to stay away. One memory, and more kisses than I ever thought I'd share with her, have proven to me what I suspected well before we reached d'Almerita.

Our bond grows deeper and deeper each day. Which is precisely why I should be in my own chamber, asleep, waiting for the son of the King of Meria to contact us. Instead, I am stalking toward Hilla's tub, completely nude now, and reaching my hand out to her.

I am impatient to see more of her, the fire and candlelight obscuring my view. Without a word, she takes my hand, and I pull her from the tub. Hilla's wet body slams against me as I claim her mouth, her breasts pressed upon my chest, her backside cupped with my hands.

I'd been prepared to enter earlier when I saw the tub being carried in. But wishing to give her sufficient time to wash, I waited. The longest wait of my life. Pacing my own small bedchamber, I envisioned this. Us. Together again.

"I need you, Hilla," I say, breaking apart from her. The words are a surprise to my own ears.

Her lips, swollen from my kiss, her arms draped around my neck, the Princess of Edingham responds by licking her lips. Tis too much. With one quick maneuver, she is in my arms. I carry her to the bed like a babe, but one fully grown. And more enticing than any woman in all the Isle.

"Aiken," she breathes, but I do not give her a chance to finish the thought. My body covers hers, my hands dipping between her legs as our mouths meld together once more.

My tongue matching the rhythm of my fingers, I do not relent as her hips move against my hand, more quickly with each thrust. I do not relent even as she begins to climax. Instead, I taste her and touch her with every bit of the desire I feel for this woman.

I will her to soar. When she does, I guide myself into her. Hilla's wetness makes slipping inside easy, and natural. Groaning, I kiss her with even greater fervor, knowing I'll not last long.

We move as one, our bodies more accustomed to each other than the first time. Knowing I must pull myself from her soon, I wait only for her to climax again. I hold fast, tensing as Hilla's breathing begins to accelerate, but the moment she gasps, jerking with a powerful thrust of her hips, I withdraw.

Shifting us away from the evidence of my need for this woman, I take her in my arms, kiss her on the head, and attempt to regain my own breath. Sometime later, I finally apologize to her.

"I will fetch you my own bed coverings."

Her laugh makes my chest swell, the sound, and the feel of her, simply too much to bear. I cannot leave. Not tonight.

Maybe not ever.

3 2

HILLA

I sit back on the bed, fully dressed, waiting for Aiken. He thought it best for me to have an escort to the hall, and after last eve, I am inclined to agree with him. There is a grittiness to the place, to Murwood End, that exists nowhere else on the Isle. Perhaps it is the dark-colored garments, the furs that are mostly absent back in Edingham except for during the height of the winter. Whatever the reason, tis a place like no other. The strength radiating from my new friend Aedre that was evident to me from the start . . . I understand it now having seen her home for the first time in years.

As it tends to do, my mind wanders back to the man who left my bed early this morn to his own bedchamber. Every day that passes, I think less and less of Whitley, of the insults and impending doom, such memories are replaced with new ones.

Replaced by thoughts of Aiken.

The feel of his lips on mine. Of how the muscles in his arms move under my fingertips as he makes love to me. Of him inside me. Of his tongue. His expression as he enters me.

So many more enjoyable thoughts, including those of our quiet conversations.

I am falling in love with a man I know little about.

While he's shared stories of his childhood, mostly of his earliest memories, there are so many gaps in his recollections. He holds back so much still. Aiken insists he is unable to tell me more. He speaks of a code, one that clearly holds more sway over him than anything else in his life. Because I see it in his eyes. As we dined last eve, he wanted to tell me more.

Although I admire the loyalty to a cause, I cannot help but get angry at times too. If he trusted me, as he claims he does, could he not just simply share his secret? As I shared mine with him? Cettina would never believe I'd done so. We agreed never to do such a thing. The knowledge could undermine her authority as queen. Could harm the very kingdom she so deftly rules, despite its many challenges.

My sister had been so angry that day, when she'd realized what I had done. When Father banished me, and my husband, naming Cettina queen, it instilled in me a resolve I had not known was possible. Despite her claims to the contrary, my sister would always have made a better queen. She was born for the role, while I prefer the shadows.

Like Aiken.

Even still, she had been furious. She'd begged me so often, especially after Father died, to return to court. To allow her to dissolve my marriage. But I'd known I could do more good as Whitley's wife than I could at Breywood, and I had been right.

A quick knock was followed by my door being opened.

"Did I not tell you to lock it behind me?" Aiken asks, entering the small chamber.

"I find my tolerance for following orders has greatly diminished as of late."

Aiken's eyes narrow as he closes, and locks, the door behind him. My heartbeat races as he moves toward me.

"I would ask next time then please do not leave your door unlocked." He reaches me. "Princess." His hand slips behind the nape of my neck. "I will never become accustomed to the idea that I am touching"—his thumb circles, caressing my skin until finally stopping, his fingers tangling in my hair —"the Princess of Edingham."

Pulling my head to his, Aiken kisses me.

And I kiss back. Hungry for him. Terrified at how much I've anticipated this moment since I woke.

His lips glide across my own in perfect rhythm until he groans, a sound I'm coming to enjoy, and pulls away.

"And I will never become accustomed to the idea that I am kissing an Elderman," I say, glancing down at his robes. "It feels quite scandalous, if I am speaking honestly."

"As it should." With a sigh, he releases his grip on my neck, takes a deep breath, and steps back. "My intention was to bring you belowstairs to break your fast. Not to accost you the moment I walked through the door."

Quite truthfully, I say, "You can accost me anytime you like, *Father* Aiken."

His eyes darken, his jaw grinding in . . . frustration?

"Do not tempt me, *Princess*."

The emerging reckless side of me answers. "Nay?"

Remembering his reaction last eve, I test my wares again. Tis an easy thing to do, showing Aiken how much I wish for him to kiss me again.

"Hilla," he growls before closing the distance between us once again. His lips, his hands, they are everywhere at once. If not for a knock on the door, I've no doubt last eve would have been repeated.

As he breaks away and makes for the door, I readjust my gown—given to me by Aiken.

Just before he opens the door, Aiken looks back at me.

"This is not finished, Hilla."

"I would hope it is not."

He smiles.

If Salvi thinks it odd to find Aiken and I alone in my bedchamber when the door is opened, he shows no hint of it.

"You may wish to come below immediately," he says, his tone urgent. "A messenger arrived, asking for you both. He will not give his missive to anyone but Father Aiken or Lady Hilla."

"A messenger," Aiken starts, and I add, "From?"

Salvi smiles and nods his head toward the corridor. We quickly follow, navigating our small party of three to the stairs. As we descend, Aiken turns to look up at me. His expression is filled with promise. With anticipation.

We are about to receive a message from the bastard son of King Galfrid. A man who could alter the course of the Isle's future as I stand witness, the supposed enemy of Meria, the daughter of a man who hated Murwood's independence nearly as much as he did all Merians. And yet, as Aiken turns away and reaches the bottom of the stairs, I think of only one thing.

If, when, and how Aiken and I will be together again.

33

AIKEN

*W*e'd been expecting a missive. Instead, Hilla and I find ourselves riding away from Sailor's Inn on borrowed mounts.

After finding us at the inn, the messenger—now riding ahead of us—gave us no time to break our fast. If we wanted to speak to Aldwine, he would escort us immediately to Nord Manor, to stay the night as his guests as we would be trapped there for the evening on the tidal island. Having spied Nord Manor as we sailed into Murwood End, we immediately understood. On the eastern edge of the village, the impressive structure is built atop a massive rock island, the base of which becomes submerged at high tide, making it impossible to come or go.

Quickly packing our bags, bidding adieu to Salvi and the others who had not received such an invitation, despite—or perhaps because of—being official representatives of the king. Hilla glances my way now as we ride down a long, wet sand path that leads up to what some might consider a small castle. Built, I've been told, by Aldwine's father. Not Galfrid, but the man who had raised him.

The sight before us is a beautiful one. The vast sea, cold and unforgiving, lies just behind the lone structure sitting atop a rock outcropping. It is an even more magnificent sight up close. But not as magnificent as the one to my left.

We rode so often together, I've rarely seen her astride a horse herself as she is now. Hilla has never looked more like a princess than this moment, except perhaps when she first entered Galfrid's throne room. Back straight, her fur-lined mantle covers both her and the borrowed mount, her hair spilling around her in every direction courtesy of the cool gusts of wind around us.

She catches me looking.

Early this morn I woke, leaving her and promising to return. But I did not do so immediately, simply dressing and taking my leave. At first, I lay in the bed, staring at the ceiling above me, thinking only one thing.

How could I leave her?

If Aldwine refuses, which we are all prepared for him to do, then I return south. To join the battle. To serve Silvester, possibly. My course is uncertain and will be determined by the Legion. Either way, tis no life for a princess, especially if I continue to play the role of Elderman.

Hilla will return to Breywood Castle, to take her rightful place as the sister of the queen. A widow beholden to no one. As she deserves.

As always, the thought of it, of us parting, feels as if my chest is being ripped open. As we make our way through the gatehouse to a small inner courtyard, I attempt to turn my attention from the woman riding by my side.

Dismounting not far from the front doors of the large manor, our horses quickly being taken away by a stablehand, we follow the Voyager who had come to fetch us. The bright morning sunlight streams in through more windows than I would expect from such a fortress. I suppose the tidal island enjoys some natural fortifications.

A servant approaches us. "Father. My lady. I would take your mantles from you. Master Aldwine is waiting abovestairs, in the solar."

With no sign now of the man who brought us here, we follow the gangly servant, who has seen no more than twenty summers, up a winding staircase. He leaves us at the entrance of the last door in a corridor so long it must run the length of the manor.

Pushing it open, the servant bids us enter.

Before learning of Kipp Aldwine's true identity, I'd already heard of the man's name many times. Rumors swirl around the Isle of the man's strength and deftness with the sword. His talent from his father, no doubt.

Dressed simply in braies and a linen tunic, he stands as we enter. No one—not King Galfrid nor even Baldric, indeed no Shadow Warrior or Voyager or any man whom I've met in my life—has made a chill sweep my body with his mere presence as this man is provoking in me now.

My eyes dart to Hilla, who is openly staring. No face is more perfect. No man's body is more finely sculpted. Awash in jealousy over the look she gives him, I am stunned as Aldwine bows deeply.

"Lady Hilla, Princess of Edingham. Welcome to Nord Manor."

She curtsies prettily as he stands straight, coming toward me.

"Father Aiken." His deference toward Hilla's station says much, especially given the man is a Voyager, not known for their deference to anyone.

"Master Aldwine."

Not even a lord, and yet, he could be king.

"Come, sit. You are most welcome."

A meal is laid out on the table closest to the hearth.

"I'm told you have not yet broken your fast?"

How could he know such a thing? Our escort arrived here along with us.

"You've spies," I guess, "at the inn."

We sit, the warmth of the fire a welcome respite from the cold. I've suddenly no desire to visit Murwood End in the winter.

"Aye. And was curious, before I spoke to Lorenson, why Silvester's man and the queen's sister had arrived with the king's messengers. Even now," he says as he pours a drink for Hilla, "I still wonder at the company you keep, my lady."

Hilla reaches for her goblet, thanking him and pulling a piece of bread onto the pewter plate in front of her.

"As do I, at times, Master Aldwine."

He laughs easily, and I cannot help but agree with d'Abella. He told me, as did Lady Aedre, Aldwine was born for the role his father wishes him to fulfill. A warrior, a gentleman, with a kindness that is evident, even though he cannot mask his unease at our presence.

"Dal said Aedre bid you to come here? Why would you help Galfrid after what he's done?" he asks Hilla.

I hold my breath waiting for her answer. Lord d'Abella, Lady Aedre, and indeed Galfrid himself were quite clear. Aldwine refused the king's summons because he hates the man for abandoning his mother. D'Abella, one of Galfrid's most trusted men and like a son to him, told me the full story before we departed.

When the queen learned of her husband's affair with one of her own ladies-in-waiting—Aldwine's mother—and insisted she and the babe leave d'Almerita, the king reluctantly agreed. He made provisions for the safety of the mother and son, hiring the most skilled swordsman of his day, a mercenary with a highly regarded reputation in both kingdoms to bring them to Murwood End.

Galfrid was pleased to learn of the marriage between his former lover and the mercenary, even more so because the man had returned the trunk of gold coin he'd been paid to escort her to Murwood End. His son would be raised by an honorable man. Throughout the years, Galfrid sent men to Murwood End to check on Kipp.

The boy was well cared for . . . until his father died in battle and his mother succumbed to the same sleeping illness that took my own parents. Aldwine has never forgiven the king for sending his mother away and blames him for her death at too young an age.

Hilla now knows this story as well and is clearly being careful with her words.

"My father was a good king for many years," she says. "He'd never been a particularly kind man, but always a good king to his people. When my mother died, he changed. Became bitter. Vengeful. After the affair that saw me banished and my sister named his successor, I cared for only one thing. Helping my sister rule the only home I'd known."

Aldwine's eyes narrow as he thinks on her words, mayhap realizing how much he and Hilla have in common.

"As I said, he was a good king, and Cettina had learned much from him. But whereas my father hated all Merians, your—" she clears her throat, "—King Galfrid included, Cettina does not. Indeed, she was quite angry that he'd sent two hundred men to Galmouth Bay. No doubt, had they landed, a bloody battle would have ensured many more years of enmity between our kingdoms."

"No doubt," Aldwine quips, clearly impatient with the topic. Each time the king is mentioned, he tenses.

Because I serve both kingdoms, I interject now. "He sent those men because of the attack on village of Saitford, where innocent Merians were killed."

Hilla looks at me, but she does not dispute it.

"We now know," I continue, the time having come for me

179

to share my own piece of the puzzle, "that attack had been facilitated, not by sanctioned forces but by renegades, to cause the very war it nearly precipitated." I take a deep breath and share my own story. "As you know from Dal Lorenson, I am not an Elderman. Few know the truth, even fewer the reason for my mission. Father Silvester has been busy these past years, securing his own continued influence. When King Malcom died and Cettina became queen, he wrongly saw an opportunity where one had not existed before."

Aldwine frowns. "Because she is a woman."

"Aye. And because he knew some in Edingham would seek to take advantage of what they saw as a weakness. You know the Highlander Lord Rawlins, I am told?"

Hilla eats in silence, listening. She knows some of this, but not all.

When I turn back to Aldwine, the look on his face startles me. If I thought his grimace at King Galfrid's name was anger, it seems I misinterpreted it. But there is no mistaking his expression now as anything but true anger, for Aldwine's knuckles are white as he grips the goblet so tight I would not be surprised if it bent beneath his fingers.

"Aye," he grinds out, "I know the man well."

Lady Aedre told me that story back at Castle d'Almerita.

Kipp holds Rawlins more responsible for his father's death than he blames Galfrid for his mother's. Indeed, Kipp commissioned a sword from my father once and told him his intention was to kill the Highlander with it someday. You see, Rawlins lost his estate and hired an army of mercenaries to gain it back. He did, at a considerable loss of life. And one of those mercenaries was Kipp's father, Sir Nicholas. Worse, he refused to pay Kipp even though he fought alongside his father, saying his agreement was with the father and not the son.

But I already knew that story. I knew Sir Nicholas had

met the man more than once. I would tell Aldwine, except that I cannot. My vow prevents it.

"Silvester sent me," I continue, "to the Tournament of Loigh to treat with men in his service. Rawlins. Lord Whitley, Hilla's late husband . . ."

Aldwine's head snaps toward Hilla.

"I had not realized Lord Whitley was dead. My condolences, Lady Hilla."

"No condolences necessary, my lord. He was not a good man and had planned to attack Craighcebor as another attempt to incite a war."

I am less delicate with my words. "The man spawned from the devil," I tell Aldwine. "His death was most welcome."

Aldwine smiles for the first time since we began our story.

"Then you have my congratulations instead," he says to Hilla.

Aldwine and I share a glance, and a bond is formed.

"I was privy," I say, continuing my story, "to their planning of the attack at Craighcebor."

Aldwine thinks on this, his questions coming quickly.

"Silvester condoned killing innocents?"

"Aye. Though he never said as much aloud, it was the only purpose for my presence at that tourney. To aid those who would cause instability between the kingdoms."

"Why?"

A trickier question. "All have their own reasons for supporting such a vile act. Some, to retaliate against Meria. Others, perhaps, to force Cettina from the throne."

Hilla shifts in her seat at that.

"But Silvester knows something the Highlanders do not. He knows how close Galfrid is to losing his crown to Hinton. Indeed, since we've returned to d'Almerita, the king and the

Prima have met, Silvester making his alliance to Hinton clear. As we sit here, the battle has likely already begun."

But he knows all this. Lord d'Abella came here just months ago to beg Aldwine to return south, to claim his inheritance. But he refused. And will do so again, most likely. Unless we can convince him otherwise.

"Lord Hinton is more malleable than Galfrid," he correctly surmises.

"Aye."

"And my sister," Hilla adds, "a more formidable queen than Silvester imagined. She is not so easily deposed."

Hilla's love and adoration for Cettina is so evident, I wonder how I'd ever misjudged her. I could almost laugh now at the idea of her plotting against the queen. The notion is more ridiculous than I could have imagined.

"I can understand," Aldwine says, "why Lord d'Abella came here. Why Galfrid sends another contingent of men. Lord Hinton's reputation precedes him. But what I do not yet understand is why the two of you are here to plead his case?"

I cannot tell him that. So I look to Hilla to answer. And she does.

"My sister and I wish only for peace. For the good of our people. And for all those on the Isle, including your own, Master Aldwine. Lady Aedre bid me to come here, saying only that I had a role to play. I know not what that role is, precisely, but I can tell you . . . we are willing to forgive that Galfrid sent his best warriors to Galmouth Bay. We will treat with him still. But we will not forge an alliance with a man like Hinton, who has many times proclaimed his dislike for those who do not hail from Meria. We will not ally with a man who would so willingly forge an alliance with Father Silvester, a man willing to sacrifice innocent men and women to further his cause."

Her shoulders rising and falling as she leans forward, her hands no longer on her lap, Hilla speaks with conviction. With the kind of passion I now know well.

Aldwine stares at her, unflinching, and Hilla stares straight back at him. How she thinks Cettina is a better choice for queen, I do not know. Her sister has shown herself to be a fine leader, but Hilla would have made just as competent a queen of Edingham.

"And you, Aiken?" He does not use the Elderman title, all pretense of it dropped. For which I am grateful. "Why are you here?" Aldwine asks, finally breaking eye contact with Hilla.

My jaw sets.

"You are not an Elderman. You plead your case for both kingdoms. Why?"

None can ever learn of your true identity. Unless a life hangs in the balance, tis a secret you will take to the grave. Vow it now or forgo your oath.

"I cannot tell you."

"You ask for me to serve a man who abandoned my mother. Who cares only of my existence because his real son, the real heir, died." A tic in his jaw reveals his annoyance. "To give up my life, one my parents built for me. My friends. My voyaging. All that I know. To do something I've not been trained for. And you will not give me your identity?"

I lift my chin, saying nothing.

"My sister had not been trained to be queen," Hilla says. "The crown was thrust upon her." Aldwine turns his head toward Hilla. "I was falsely accused of having an affair and tossed from all that I'd known to live with a cruel man who blamed me for his misfortune. When my father died, I did not run back to Breywood, even though Cettina offered to grant me a divorce. Instead, I remained with Whitley, fed my sister much-needed information from the men who would plot against her. I did it for her, for Edingham. For the good of the people who would have suffered had I looked only to my own comforts."

I love her.

I love this woman. Have loved her for some time. The revelation is not a welcome one, but tis true nonetheless.

Aldwine says nothing in response to her, turning to me instead.

"Who are you?"

I brace myself and answer, "I would break a vow by telling you."

Aldwine is remarkably calm as I continue to deny him. He looks from me to Hilla.

"I know not either," she says. "He has not told me."

I hate the pain in her voice as she speaks those words. But there is no help for it.

Suddenly, Aldwine shoots to his feet. I think he means to toss us from this solar chamber. Instead, he paces, his hands covering his face as he walks in circles. He stops to look at Hilla and then resumes his pacing. Making his way to the window, Aldwine tosses open the wooden shutters. Cursing, he ignores us as Hilla and I exchange an uneasy glance.

When he finally turns back to us, I am surprised to see him smiling.

"If you tell me, I will go with you."

Hilla gasps.

"If you do not, I will remain here. Lives will be lost in the ensuing battle for Galfrid's throne."

"A fact you knew already, before we came here," I say.

"A fight," he says, "that is not mine. But you miss the point of my condition, Aiken. Lives will be lost if you do not reveal your identity. As I very much intend to remain in Murwood End otherwise."

My hand freezes on the goblet I'd been about to drink from.

He knows.

"Say it, Aiken. You break no vow in doing so."

I must be sure. "If I do not tell you, then you remain in Murwood End? But if I reveal myself, you will return with us to Meria? To claim your title as heir to the King of Meria?"

It seems Hilla had something to do with this stunning reversal. He looks at her, Hilla completely bewildered now, and winks. "I have been convinced to do so, aye."

I've not once said the words aloud. But the condition has been met, and so I brace myself and speak my truth.

"I am a member of the Legion of Ash."

34

HILLA

*N*ay, it cannot be.

Aiken avoids looking at me, and I am glad for it. If Aldwine's words were true, the future of this Isle may have just been altered in this chamber. And yet, I can think of nothing beyond Aiken's revelation.

Aldwine echoes my own thoughts.

"That cannot be. There is no longer a Legion of Ash."

Aiken does not refute him, but tis clear, he is not jesting. How is this possible?

"I know better than most, for my father was a member many, many years ago, in his youth. But they've disbanded, their power having grown too strong. He told me himself, the last time the Legion met was . . ."

"When Silvester came to power," Aiken finishes. "As Second, he wielded more influence than any second in power before him. If you'll remember, the loudest calls crying foul at the Legion's influence came from the very man I now supposedly serve."

His words ring true. At least, from the stories I have

heard. As he talks, I think of all I know about the Legion of Ash. After Athea assisted Lady Edina in making a potion for King Onry to fall in love with her, and after Edina and Onry's sons split the Isle into two kingdoms, many blamed the Garra. At the height of that backlash, a woman was burned at the stake in Firley Dinch, a village at the border between the two kingdoms. It was later learned the woman was no Garra at all but an innocent.

In their fervor, she and her unborn babe were put to death. From the ashes of her body there rose an order of men intent on forbidding such an atrocity to recur. Some say these men became the greatest warriors in the Isle, even greater than the Shadow Warriors, from their sheer will to see such an injustice never happen again. Others say their unnatural abilities stemmed from their alliance with the Garra.

Aided by the healers, the Legion of Ash grew so strong that, years later, calls for them to disband echoed throughout the Isle. And they did. Or so most believed. There have been whispers of a new, secret order made up of former Legion members, but none have seen evidence of such a thing.

Until now.

"A Shadow Warrior *and* a member of the Legion of Ash," I say bitterly, my hands shaking at the revelation, one Aiken never hinted at. I look at him now and realize I know the man not at all, despite the intimacies we've shared. "You are quite a warrior, *Father* Aiken."

I've no patience for his look of regret, of sadness. He could have told me but did not. Instead, he trusts a man he's never met with the information instead.

"There is no longer a Legion of Ash," Aldwine repeats, seemingly not hearing the exchange between Aiken and me. "My father would have known of it."

As the morning stretches on, the fire crackling next to us, the world as we know it shifting beneath our feet, Aiken pushes back his wooden seat. Suddenly, I hate his robes. The lying. The deceit. I am in love with a man I do not know.

Casting my eyes away, I look toward the fire as he speaks to Aldwine.

"He did know of it," Aiken says softly. "I knew your father. Met him on more than one occasion."

In spite of myself, I look back to the men just in time to see Aldwine's stunned expression.

"After Silvester was named Prima, the Legion made a show of disbanding. Your father, as did many others, joined a mercenary company. Legion members consist of noblemen, innkeepers, mercenaries, even Eldermen..."

"Real Eldermen?" I ask, unable to keep the bitterness from my voice.

Aiken's piercing gaze does naught to calm the erratic beating of my heart. "Aye. Real Eldermen," he says wryly.

"We took our meeting places underground, allowing the belief that we were no longer together to persevere. But I can assure you," he addresses Aldwine, "we have not stopped working for the good of the Isle."

We took our meeting places underground.

"The tavern in d'Almerita?" I ask, already knowing the answer.

"Aye."

"My father continued to serve the Legion," Aldwine says, sitting back down at the table. "The Legion protects the Garra, preserves peace."

"Aye," Aiken agrees.

"Which of his missions throughout the years were in service to the Legion?"

Aiken sighs heavily. "I cannot tell you that. But I will tell you, Sir Nicholas was a highly respected warrior who saved many lives."

Aldwine's elbows rest on the table. He wipes his eyes, as if to clear his thoughts, and then rests his face in his hands, saying nothing.

"Your close friendship with Lady Aedre . . ." Aiken drifts off, not continuing the unfinished thought.

"She knew?" Aldwine asks.

Aiken shakes his head. "Nay. Not even the Garra we protect know of our true identity. At least, not all of them. I suspect her grandmother might have known."

At least I'm not the only one.

"We are bound to a vow of secrecy. Unless a life is threatened. I heard a story from one of the men who trained me about a Garra in Murwood End who owed her life to your father. Likely he was forced to tell Aedre's grandmother because her life had been threatened in some way. Your family's bond to hers—"

"Is not simply because Aedre's mother and mine were dear friends." Aldwine shoves his drink away and jumps to his feet. "I need something stronger than this." He walks to a cupboard, grabs a vessel and pours. "Wine, anyone?"

Aiken and I exchange a glance.

"By now the tide will have risen. I keep a boat and can get you to the mainland, but with all that has transpired here this morn, I propose we drink instead. Stay as my guests."

I would prefer to leave. To sail away from Murwood End, away from Aiken, and back to Edingham. To reunite with Cettina, tell her all that has transpired, and embrace my sister, never letting go. Never leaving my home again.

But there is more to learn, and plans to be made that I must communicate to Cettina when I do go back. Because the fantasies that have begun to dance around in my head, thoughts of remaining with Aiken, have been proven to be nothing more than silly notions of a woman who still has much to learn.

It seems I know little of this Isle on which I live, and even less of the man I gave myself to, twice. I should at least learn of the former before I return to Cettina. And the latter?

Silvester can have him.

35

AIKEN

*A*s I wait for the others, Hilla lagging behind with Salvi and Kipp—no longer Master Aldwine to me after a day of drinking and an evening of conversation that seems a lifetime ago even though it has been just a day—I watch Voyagers come and go. One ship prepares to depart for Stoughrock, an island north of Murwood with whom they trade. Others, to fish, and still other ships, I know not their destination.

Our own is now prepared to set sail for Meria.

The docks are so different here than in the south. One isle, and yet here it is cold, the people independent. In Meria, the warmth begets flowers not seen anywhere else on the Isle. In the east there lies the mountains of the Highlands, some as cold and unforgiving as Murwood End, and others closer to the southeast, more green.

When Kipp asked how I'd joined the Legion, though Hilla pretended not to listen, I know she hung on every word. Unfortunately, she's not done so since. Instead, Hilla has refused to speak to me. She even asked Salvi to show her

Murwood the day after we returned from Nord Manor. He was glad to do it, and seemed even to revel in the attention.

For my part, I drank myself into a stupor, something I've not done in many years. After I woke the next day, Hilla refusing to break her fast with me, I returned to Nord as Kipp requested. There, we plotted and planned. I shared every bit of my knowledge of Galfrid's court, of Silvester and his machinations as well as all the information I'd gathered these past months about Hinton. He worried over the man whom Galfrid had named his successor, Lord Calderone. I assured him that the king's distant relative had no designs on the throne other than to waylay Lord Hinton.

When Kipp returned, he would be welcome by Galfrid, by his men, and by many in Meria. But I did not shy away from telling him of all those who supported Hinton's claim. The nobles who stood to gain from the man's empty promises. And how Silvester had turned from the king toward a man he thought could serve him better. That was, for me, the most concerning of all.

Kipp Aldwine was returning to Meria to claim his rightful place as King Galfrid's successor.

And yet here I stand, thinking of what I will say to Hilla on the voyage back. If I've not been ruthless in my pursuit of her these past few days, it is because her anger is justified. I take her to my bed, love her in the only way I can, and tell her nothing of the most important part of me. The part, as I told Kipp with Hilla listening, that had been awakened all those years ago.

The son of a woman who sold her body for coin, a skinny boy who only learned to fight after he was beaten so badly his eyes would not open for nearly two days. A boy with no hope for the future, whose fists were his only salvation.

It was that boy Baldric found one fateful day. Curious at the shouts, he watched me fight a man who had mistreated my mother. By then, my skinny arms were muscled, and my resolve, which had been there since the day years earlier when I could hear my mother's voice but could not open my swollen eyes to see her, evident to Baldric. Or so he told me later.

Not one of the men in the Legion of Ash was recruited in the same way. Some, like Roger Orazio, became members because of their fathers. But not all sons did so, only those with the most potential.

Some came with no knowledge of how to use their fists, or the sword, but whose loyalty had been tested, and proven, in some way. Others, like me, just the opposite. Baldric watched me for a long time. Finally convinced I was worthy, he approached my mother first. By the time she spoke to me, I had little choice but to go with him. I was a man fully grown by then. But when the woman who gave you birth begs for something—the possibilities Baldric had shown her enough to overcome the worry that she'd see me little over the coming years—a man has little choice.

So I went with him, trained with him, and eventually, years later, said the oath that bound me to the men I now call brothers. Ones, like Baldric, for whom I would lay down my life ten times over if need be.

Few of the Legion had wives, although there was no vow against it. But what woman would readily agree to the kind of life I am bound to until death? Not always remaining at one place for long, nearly always in danger. I'd never ask such a thing of any woman, most especially a princess.

Hilla belonged at court, with her sister. Comfortable. Protected. Safe.

And so what could I say to her? That I'd not meant to fall in love with her? That I was sorry for not telling her the truth? It would be another lie. I am not sorry for a vow that prevents me from sharing my identity. Being a member of the Legion of Ash has been my greatest achievement. I'd sooner toss myself from this dock with my leg weighted than break that vow.

Firmus maneo. I remain steadfast. Even as the woman I love walks toward me now. Still, I know not what to say to her, but at least she cannot avoid me aboard a ship for more than a fortnight.

Not far behind her trail Salvi and the other men.

"Do you always brood so, Aiken?"

I'd not seen Kipp approaching. For a man with my training, being caught unaware is unusual. And yet, until his hand clasps my shoulder, I'd not seen him coming.

"Where did you come from?"

Kipp crosses his arms. To think just days ago we were strangers.

"You are not the only one with skills, Father."

His tone implies a knowledge he alone possesses. Like Hilla when she first learned of it, Kipp seems eager to overuse my title now that he is aware.

"A good thing, as you will need them very soon."

Hilla.

She reaches us, greets Kipp more warmly than me, and turns to speak to Salvi.

When I asked Kipp that day as we drank more wine than should be drunk in one sitting what had convinced him when so many others failed before us, it was Hilla he spoke of. Her sacrifice for Cettina had moved him.

He'd been thinking of Aedre's safety as continued rumors of a battle between Galfrid and Hinton grew. Still, he remained in Murwood, angry with his father and unwilling to help him. But when Hilla told the story of how she'd remained married to aid her sister, something snapped inside him, or so Kipp explained. He could, and should, sacrifice the stubbornness that held him back from what he knew he had to do.

Apparently Kipp had been more opposed to giving his father something he desired than he was to ruling a kingdom. That, he admitted later, was daunting but not as much so as allowing Galfrid into his life.

Somehow, Aedre had known Hilla's influence would be needed. I long ago stopped questioning the Garra's ways. Having helped to protect them for many years, my appreciation for their beliefs, their powers, only continues to grow.

"We will meet again in d'Almerita, Father Aiken," Kipp says now. I shake the hand of the future king of Meria. Some may think my sentiments are premature. Hinton has promised coin, land and influence to enough men to make him a serious threat, even without the church's backing. And yet, what else is there to do but hope, lest faith turn to despair.

"I thank you for making the journey here," he says, waving to someone in the distance. "I look forward to seeing you again."

"Under much different circumstances, to be sure," Hilla responds.

Kipp leans in toward me and whispers, "She is worth fighting for, Aiken."

With that, he turns to walk away. Not once have we spoken of my love for Hilla. My feelings for her must not be as well hidden as I thought. Turning to find Salvi standing at my back, I greet him and the other men.

"'Tis time," I say, looking back at the village, at the inn where I spent a most glorious night with a woman who refuses to look at me now. "Come, Hilla, the captain waves to us even now."

She does not move.

"Hilla?"

She looks at me with such sadness, such despair, that my heart surely just stops beating. Nay, it cannot be.

"The Talisman sails to Breywood." She nods to a trading ship docked nearby.

"No." I pull her away from the edge of the dock, toward a small wooden building that serves as a lookout. "No Hilla, you cannot."

She lifts her chin. "I am no longer your captive, Aiken."

Wincing at her words, I refuse to believe it. "You do not speak to me for days, and now you will leave like this? Without so much as a fare-thee-well? I do not know that ship's captain. You will not sail unattended with strangers, Hilla."

They were, apparently, the wrong words.

"I am the daughter of King Malcom Borea of Edingham, sister to the queen, Princess of Edingham and direct descendant of the son of King Onry. You will not tell me where, or with whom, I can sail."

I take a step back, looking at Hilla as if we have just met. In some ways, it feels very much as if she is a stranger to me. Her strength . . . it has always been there, of course. But she is not the same woman that I took at Craighcebor.

"The captain," she says, "is a friend of Kipp's. He has offered his protection. You may ask him if you wish."

My gaze shoots to Kipp, who is still on the docks speaking to a group of men.

Traitor.

"I begged him not to tell you. I knew you might convince me to sail back with you."

She is worth fighting for, Aiken.

So he does not have the sight of the Garra, and perhaps I've not made my feelings for Hilla obvious after all. He knew because she sought his help. His protection. To sail away from me.

"Why, Hilla?"

Her eyes are strong, and clear. Tis obvious she's given the matter much thought.

"Because I love you, Aiken."

The answer nearly fells me as if she struck me with a sword, and I am unarmed and unprepared for such an attack.

"How I can love a man I did not truly know, I am still uncertain. But with you, my resolve is weak. Had I told you my plans, and had you asked for me to join you, I would have done so."

So there is hope still. "Then come with me now. We can speak on the journey. Do not leave this way, Hilla."

She is resolved. I know it from the way she stands before me.

"What would we speak of? Our future together?"

I blink, unsure as ever what to say.

"I do not stay in any place for long," I admit. "And am often surrounded by danger."

"Go on, Aiken. Say it."

I cannot. I will not.

"Tis no place for a woman, for a wife, by your side. Ahem is that what you wish to say?" she goads, and I take the bait.

"How often were you put in danger on this journey?"

"And yet, I am here. Hearty and well," she snaps back.

"You should be at court," I argue, "safe and well protected."

"Aye? Is that where I belong?"

"Hilla . . ."

"What would you say to me, Aiken? Shall we prolong our goodbyes until after I land in Meria, in the midst of a war?"

Grinding my teeth together so hard my jaw hurts, I say nothing. She is a princess. I am no more than a mercenary, albeit one who fights for something more than coin. I fight for peace, for love. For all that Hilla wishes for this Isle. But I say nothing, because she is right. It is selfish of me to want to extend our goodbye when neither of us know what Meria will bring. Even if Hinton has besieged the capital, it would be safe still. But would it be safer for her to avoid it? Aye.

Can I have a future with the Princess of Edingham? Nay.

Tell her you love her anyway.

It will only make our parting more difficult. She is right. Hilla is best off to go home now.

"So this is where we part?"

She simply watches me in response, as if I should say more. Instead, I laugh.

"You've learned more from me than I would like, Hilla," I say, referring to her silence. But clearly, she misunderstands. And I think of us, our limbs entangled, sleeping beside one another. Can I let her walk away, to board a ship bound for Breywood? This battle could take months, years even.

"I truly hope Kipp is successful. He will find friends at Breywood eager to treat with him. With his people," she says sadly.

Tis something, at least. It seems as if a new path for the Isle, not only for Meria alone, may have been forged if Hinton can be held off. Even so, never in my life, not on the streets as a young child, not standing before Silvester, worried my identity may have been discovered, not during my training, never has my chest felt so heavy. As if my life's blood was being drained from my body.

"Farewell, Aiken."

This is not happening. Instead of saying nay and reaching out and embracing her, begging her to come with me, I remain steadfast. As I've been trained to do.

"Farewell, Hilla."

We stand there for a moment longer, Hilla's resolve as evident now as it was when we began conversing. She is leaving.

Before Kipp boards, I would speak to him. To ensure her safe passage for myself.

I lift the cowl of my robes, wanting to hide behind it. Wanting it to shield me from the pain of a loss so great I know my love is true, for nothing could possibly make a man's heart ache this way otherwise.

When I walk away, she lets me go.

36

HILLA

"Oh," I say, having been looking at Aiken and not ahead of me. "I do apologize."

The young woman I so rudely crashed into smiles warmly.

"Tis quite alright, my lady."

I move to walk past her, toward the ship where the captain Kipp introduced me to yesterday afternoon is waiting, when she stops me.

"If I may, Lady Hilla," she says, startling me by using my name.

Like most everyone here in Murwood End, I can tell little about her. Wrapped in a fur-lined mantle, she could be a servant or a lady herself. Unlike in Edingham, most everyone here wears much the same type of clothing. An idea I find rather appealing.

"Word has spread quickly," she explains. "We are rarely host to a princess here in Murwood End."

Shouts from the docks and the bustle of presailing activity surround us. Living on the coast most of my life, I've spent surprisingly little time dockside and find I quite like it here. The smell of sea air, coupled with evidence of life, the vibrancy of activity . . . tis something I vow to do when I return home.

With an escort, of course.

Unlike here in Murwood End, I'll not have the freedom to walk about unescorted as I've done these past months with Aiken. All will know me at Breywood, and 'twould not be safe to wander anywhere alone but the castle grounds, much less the docks.

In some ways, I'll be trapped again, as I've been as Whitley's wife.

We are rarely host to a princess here in Murwood End.

It was inevitable I would be recognized by someone. But this woman's home is not just host to a princess. What will she think to learn Murwood has been, for many years, home to a king? I've no doubt, with men like Lord d'Abella and Aiken, as well as the other Legion members who Aiken said would fight for him, that Hinton's uprising will fail. And that Kipp will be named the successor to King Galfrid.

"I do wish I could have remained here in Murwood End for longer. It is a most delightful place." Delightful, and a tad bit scary as well. I'm certain tis my imagination, but the men seem... bigger. Their weapons certainly are so. The customs, very different than in the south.

"I bid you a safe journey," she says. "There is naught like the feeling of going home, aye?"

I cock my head, thinking on that.

"My father was a Voyager," she explains. "I've been everywhere on the Isle, and on trade routes north and east, with him."

"That must have been exciting," I say, thinking of Aiken's words. He is so convinced I am too delicate for his life that he did not once consider I might enjoy such a thing.

"Aye, very much. But my days of traveling the Isle are

over. I am married, with a babe. And as the only midwife here in Murwood since Lady Aedre left, I'm needed here."

"You knew Lady Aedre?"

"She and her grandmother trained me."

What a woman Aedre's grandmother must have been. "I met her at Castle d'Almerita, before coming here. She is truly a wonder."

"Aye, she is that. A stronger woman I've never met."

"It is because of her that I came here," I admit.

The woman's eyes widen. "I do hope your journey has been successful."

In some ways, it has. More than this stranger will ever know. In others, it has been just the opposite. I will forever remember Murwood End as the place where I lost Aiken forever. Aye, 'twas my choice to part from him. After my anger abated, I realized having Aiken break a vow to tell me of his identity would make him a different man than I know him to be. But while I could appreciate his steadfastness and loyalty, our circumstances were no less altered, our future together no more hopeful.

What would happen if I sailed to Meria with him? We would be intimate on the journey south, of that I have no doubt. And my love for him would only grow. Parting from him would thus be an even sweeter sorrow than if we had simply said our goodbyes now.

And yet, letting him walk away from me had been the most difficult thing I've done in my life.

"It has," I say as the captain waves to me. "I must be going. . . . I do not know your name?"

"Aloisa, my lady."

"I am pleased to make your acquaintance, Aloisa. Good day," I tell her as she smiles once again and departs. Making my way to the ship, I resist the urge to see if Aiken has departed. As I walk across the wooden plank and board the ship that will take me back to Cettina, I consider the midwife's words.

There is naught like the feeling of going home, aye?

There was a time, not long ago, I'd have wanted nothing more than to return to my sister, to the safety of Breywood. But now?

I look, in spite of myself.

He is gone.

How is it possible that Aiken's ship could have set sail already? He must have boarded quickly and departed without delay. I stare at the empty space where it was moored just moments ago. Tis gone.

And if I've any doubts about my decision, they matter naught now.

Aiken has departed, and it is unlikely I shall ever see him again.

"*We* are pulling away soon," Kipp says as his men prepare to depart.

When I inquired after Kipp about the ship he arranged for Hilla, he reassured me she would be safe. And he invited me to sail with him to Meria, rather than travel aboard the ship I'd arrived on. We hadn't considered the possibility earlier since I'd planned to visit Silvester upon returning. But Kipp was finally successful in dissuading me from meeting him again.

"Tis done," he'd said. "You've gathered as much information as you can from the man, but seeing him again . . . you could very well be marking your own death. Do you have any doubt how he would punish you if your disguise were uncovered?"

I did not. Hiding behind his robes and the vows to God he's taken, Father Silvester was as ruthless as any man I've met. A lifetime of abuse at the hands of his own father, and a need to be in control of all those around him because of it, coupled with an unmatched ambition, made him the most dangerous of any threat to this Isle.

"When will you ditch those robes?" he whispers to me now in passing.

"When I can find something more suitable to wear," I say, grabbing ahold of the mast beside me.

"Will you be glad to abandon the ruse?"

I watch as Hilla's ship prepares for departure.

"Very glad," I admit.

Kipp follows my gaze.

"Why did you let her go?"

Breathing in the salt air, I say nothing for some time. The strong breeze nearly pulls my cowl back.

"She let me go," I admit finally. "My world is not one for a princess."

"Hmm. Being raised with Edrys, and Aedre . . . I've thoughts of love more unique than most men."

I tear my gaze from Hilla to look at the man who will be king of Meria.

"Take that damn hood down. I cannot see you under it, Aiken."

Laughing, wondering what Baldric would think of Kipp's boldness, and knowing, as surely as I know my own name, that he would think fondly of Kipp, I do take it down. Blocking out the world is the only part of being an Elderman I will miss.

"Unique thoughts of love?" I ask, in spite of myself.

"In Murwood, we don't marry for advantage. There is no ruler—"

"Some would argue you have assumed that role."

He ignores me.

"No need for pretense. For posturing. We aid each other. We survive together. And . . . we love. Without apologies."

Assuming Kipp does know my feelings for Hilla, I still have little notion what the Voyager ways have to do with the princess and me.

"Surely you must know, having given your life to their protection, the Garra notions of love?"

I watch Hilla as she speaks to the captain, not once looking back.

"They believe it has the power to heal," I say. "They resist the idea the Isle was broken because of love. They believe that Lady Edina would have found a way to be with King Onry if they were fated to be together. They say, instead, the Isle will become one again only because of love, not that it was broken because of it."

"Do you believe them?" he asks.

I think of my mother then, of the many men she has been with. She does not believe in love. To her, it is a liability for her profession. But what of my own notions of love?

"I know not. I've had too few examples of love," I admit, unable to take my eyes from Hilla.

"Master Baldric and Lady Hilla excluded?" he asks.

She turns this way, finally. Looks at the dock where Salvi and the others departed moments ago. I cannot see her expression from this distance. But I can see that she continues to stare at that spot.

"What are your unique notions precisely, Kipp?" I turn from Hilla to look at him.

"I believe in the power of love, as Aedre does and Edrys before her. I've been witness to its strength. To its ability to overcome obstacles. Someday, I will love as intensely as Aedre and Vanni. As my parents loved one another." He blinks. "As you love the woman you're letting sail away."

"I do not let her sail away. Hilla has her own mind. This is her choice."

"Why do you believe she made such a choice?"

When I turn back, Hilla still stares at where the Merian ship had been. Her shoulders sag. She is sad. I do not need to see her face to know it.

"I asked Hilla that very question."

Kipp does not answer. Because he likely already knows. Only a fool could not see it.

Would she have come with me? Given up life at court to travel the Isle, more often in danger than not. For me?

Aye. She would have. I know why she made the choice to leave, because she told me.

Because I love you, Aiken.

HILLA

*T*hankful for my own cabin, and that my trunk made its way safely here courtesy of Kipp's men, I open it and peer inside. Lifting the gown that lies on top, I think of how I mistakenly assumed Galfrid had it sent to me.

Aiken. How does the Legion of Ash afford him enough coin to purchase such a gown? I never asked him that, or of other vows he may have taken when he joined. Or what his training was like. Or of his other missions.

Could he even share such information with me? Now that I know of the Legion, Aiken pleaded with me to keep the secret safe. He asked that I not even share with Cettina, and though I've never kept secrets from my sister before, I gave him my promise.

My cheeks begin to tingle, the sting of tears not far behind. I stand, determined not to cry. It will not reunite me with Aiken. But even as I will it otherwise, a single tear escapes. I wipe it away, take a deep breath, and place the gown back inside the trunk. Pulling up on my surcoat, also given to me by Aiken, I wriggle out of it, now adept at undressing without the assistance of a maid. I lay that too inside the trunk.

I should have gone above to see us off, but I wish to be alone with my thoughts. But as a knock on the door interrupts them, it seems my quiet solitude has come to an end.

I open the door, expecting to find one of the men the captain introduced me to on deck, only to be startled into a shocked silence by my visitor. Aiken is at my door, staring back at me. No mantle. No robes. Just . . . Aiken.

"What—"

I am unable to finish as Aiken propels me into the small cabin. He closes the door behind him and kisses me, so fiercely and thoroughly I cannot resist kissing him back. Aiken's mouth moves over mine, his hands holding my head in place.

Despite the tangle of tongues and caresses I'd not normally willingly stop, I find the strength to push him away.

"You left." Clearly it is not so, but I do not understand.

"Salvi and the others left," Aiken says, his hand still holding the nape of my neck as if I would attempt to escape. Maybe once I would have done so, but I do not wish to be anywhere but here just now.

"I sail with Kipp." He looks into my eyes. "We sail with Kipp."

My heart lurches at his words.

"Aiken . . ."

"Come to Meria with me. I will ensure your safety there."

"And afterward?" I keep him from pulling me in by resting a hand on his forearm, knowing if I do not do so I will agree to this journey with him.

"Afterward, you will come with me, wherever my next mission. As my wife."

He is not jesting.

"I love you, Hilla. My life is not one fit for a princess. It is dangerous. And will always be so. Until we have children, my missions will take us all over the Isle. You may not see your sister for some time. And after a babe is born, I will be gone for too-long stretches, as the Legion needs me." Words spill from his mouth. "If you would have such a life, I would be honored to be called your husband."

My body craves his touch, so instead of answering, I pull him toward me.

I love you, Hilla.

Show me, I wish to say. But I cannot. Our mouths are melded together, as if made for each other. My hands, of their own accord, tug on Aiken's linen shirt. I wish to feel him, to be closer to the man who will be my husband.

In response, he lifts both my gown and chemise. It seems Aiken understands my intent and responds in kind. When he is freed, I wrap my hands around him, reveling in the way a simple touch could make a man, a warrior, like Aiken groan in response.

Whirling us around so that my back is now against the wall, Aiken holds my gown up with one hand and guides himself inside me with the other.

"Here?" I ask, knowing I've initiated this but unsure if such a thing is possible. "The men will want to sail."

"Then let them," he growls as he enters me. Now fully inside, Aiken braces his hands on both sides of my head, against the wall. At that angle, he feels different . . . good, but different. And his face. I've never seen that expression on him before.

Aye, mayhap I have once. That day we met.

"Aiken," I manage before he moves within me. "Do you remember the day we met?"

My hands on his broad shoulders, Aiken moves and I circle my hips.

"I can't seem to recall it," he says, his eyes hooded.

Thrusting harder each time, we rise together. And even as the sensations intensify, I'm somehow able to still find my voice.

At least, I thought I could speak, but as he moves faster, harder, my core clenches. I try to warn him, knowing what comes next. Instead, he looks at me and continues to circle and thrust, Clearly has no intention of pulling himself from me.

I nod just as my whole body shudders. Squeezing his eyes shut, Aiken roars with pleasure. I never answered his question with words, but I think he knows what my answer is anyway. My head lowers to Aiken's chest as he cradles me, still joined. Our bodies recover just as a knock at the door drags us back to reality.

"Are you going with the Elderman or sailing with us, my lady?" a voice calls from the other side.

Lifting my head up, I smile and answer him clearly.

"I will not be sailing with you this morn. A moment, if you will, as I gather my belongings."

Silence greets us as his answer.

"What did you say to him?" I ask.

Aiken pulls away from me as my gown drops. I watch him as he dresses, still in disbelief about what has just transpired.

"Spy something interesting, Princess?"

My eyes fly upward. "Perhaps."

He leans in, kissing me gingerly, and then steps back. "I gave him more than enough coin to compensate for the delay and told him you'd no longer be sailing with him this morn."

"Coin from the Legion?" I ask. "I always did wonder about that."

"Aye," he says, moving toward my trunk. "Mercenaries are paid for their skill. And none are better than my brothers."

"And you."

Not a boastful man, he does not answer, so I ask another question. "How did you know I would come with you?"

"The same way I knew you would not run away at the stream that first day."

I think back, remembering. "You never did answer me then. Or most often, as I think on it. You spoke so little."

"And you, so often," he teases.

It seemed as if Aiken would lift my trunk, but instead he navigates around it and makes his way back to me. Tucking a strand of hair behind my ear, he does answer me now.

"I knew you'd not run away because you were scared." His kiss is soft, gentle. "And I knew you would come with me today because you are not. You were brave when we met, Hilla, and are even more so now. It is one of the many things I love about you. I will spend the journey back telling you all that I love about you, but I do believe tis time to leave this cramped cabin."

"For an equally cramped one on Kipp's ship?"

"Hmm." His hand slides upward from my waist, until it completely covers my breast. "Mayhap I do not mind. I've never been more anxious for a journey as I am for this one."

He squeezes gently, as if showing me what is to come.

"Cettina will think I'm mad when she learns of how we met. Tis ridiculous if you think on it. Taken by an Elderman."

The glint in his eyes hints at mischievousness. "In more ways than one."

EPILOGUE

Aiken

"*A*re you ready?" I ask as land appears on the horizon. Kipp stands beside me, the day as calm as any we've seen thus far, both of us aware the events on shore will be anything but.

"As ready as a man can be for such a thing."

He appears thoughtful. And though we know nothing of what to expect when we make port, my mission will be getting Hilla and Kipp safely ashore so Galfrid can officially declare him his heir. With luck, if the fighting has not begun, King Galfrid's proclamation, something he has been trying to achieve since his son perished, will prevent a war.

Merian law is clear. Bastard or no, Kipp Aldwine can be named the next king, his succession over Lord Hinton undeniable. Whether or not Hinton and his allies, including Silvester, will accept it, I do not know.

Since we will be separated on land, I ask him the one thing I've wondered this whole journey. A question I should not ask, but my curiosity has grown too great.

"Why did you not accept Galfrid's offer until now? You knew Hinton's plan. And must have known his rule would be detrimental to all those in Meria, and mayhap Murwood End as well?"

Kipp stares out to sea as I think of what d'Abella told me of him. Of how Kipp was the first man in a long while to best him with the sword. He possesses the blood of kings. The training of the Legion courtesy of his other father. A lifetime of the Garra's influence. The fierceness of a Voyager.

My brothers in the church—not the corrupt ones, like Silvester, but those who truly live God's words—would say he has been blessed. That his divine duty lies in Meria. True, or nay, I know only that Kipp Aldwine will be king. I am to see to it, no mission in my lifetime more important.

"Lady Hilla's sacrifice," he says finally, echoing the words he spoke back at Nord Manor.

"Influenced your decision, aye. But that does not explain why you refused before, knowing the stakes in doing so."

"I have hated two men in my life," he says, the normally affable expression on Kipp's face twisted into a grimace. "Lord Rawlins for getting my father killed. As a mercenary, Father knew each mission could be his last. But that fight was not for honor or love or loyalty. It was for a man to regain the land he lost fairly. I had no need of his coin, but that he refused to give it, even though I'd fought alongside my father . . ."

He trails off, but no words are needed. I would have slayed the man three times over for such a misdeed. Baldric would have chastised me for it, aye. But I'd have done so anyway.

"And Galfrid," he says. "Aedre would remind me that he provided for my mother and me, sending us away with more coin than we would need in a lifetime. And that 'twas my mother's choice to hie all the way north to Murwood End.

And that by giving us protection, I gained a loving father in Sir Nicholas." He turns to me. "She would be right. All of that is true. But he sent us away. If Prince Matteo had not died, I would not be on this ship sailing toward d'Almerita."

Rejection from his father kept Kipp away. It was more powerful than any sense of duty he'd felt to people he did not know. Except . . .

"And when Aedre and her father moved south?"

Surely he wanted to protect them, two people he loved now living in Meria.

He takes a deep breath, remaining silent as my wife makes her way toward us.

"So serious," she says, approaching. "What do you two speak of that has Kipp looking as if he will soon toss himself overboard?"

I reach for Hilla and pull her to my side, kissing her so thoroughly that she attempts to wriggle away, likely uncomfortable because of Kipp's presence. The first time I kissed her this way, with witnesses, was after our exchange of vows. She attempted to pull away then too, her cheeks pink. Until Kipp laughed and told her not to stop on his account. He told her later that few Voyagers abided by the protocols that encumbered those in the south, lumping Meria and Edingham together, something only a person from Murwood End would do.

"We must embrace Kipp's ways," I say as we break apart, though I do not let her go. My arm, a regular fixture on Hilla's waist, stays firmly in place. "When he is king, Murwood's customs will find their way to Meria."

"And as allies," she says, the idea of a united Isle something all three of us have spoken about at length on this journey, "to Edingham as well. But that does not mean I am suddenly accustomed to such customs already."

I wink at Kipp. "She cannot even say the word," I tell him.

"I can," she retorts back. "Kissing," she blurts. "That does not mean I am suddenly accustomed to kissing in front of others."

Kipp laughs, his mood improved now that Hilla has arrived. "We do much more than that," he says, his expression once again turning serious. "In Murwood End, it is not uncommon for men and women to make love with others present to watch."

Poor Hilla. Her cheeks already enflamed, mouth open, she simply stares.

I do believe Kipp is teasing my wife, but it is difficult to tell. He is as skilled as any in masking his true intentions when necessary. Although, I've not heard of such a custom myself.

"'Tis true," he continues. "We are not ashamed of that which brings us pleasure."

Unable to discern whether he jests with my wife or not, for her sake, I switch topics. "It seems you will bring many changes to Meria with you, Kipp. Public displays of affection included."

As Castle d'Almerita looms larger in front of us, the man who would be king looks to his future home.

"Many changes indeed," he says, "but first, we must win a war."

"And we shall," I say taking Hilla into my arms as we stare out at the castle together. Whatever the future holds for Meria, my wife and I shall weather it together.

HER VOYAGER KING, the conclusion to the Kingdoms of Meria series, is coming this June! Pre-order it here so you don't miss the special release price.

GET BOOK BONUSES

Get book bonuses by subscribing to updates for future books and other updates, including Cecelia's bi-weekly "Top 5" picks.

SIGN UP HERE

ABOUT THE AUTHOR

Cecelia Mecca is the author of medieval romance, including the Border Series, and sometimes wishes she could be transported back in time to the days of knights and castles. Although the former English teacher's actual home is in Northeast Pennsylvania where she lives with her husband and two children, her online home can be found at Cecelia-Mecca.com. She would love to hear from you.

- Subscribe to be a CM Insider to receive book news and updates via email.

Connect with Cecelia on:

ALSO BY CECELIA MECCA

Order of the Broken Blade

The Blacksmith ◆ The Mercenary

The Scot ◆ The Earl ◆ The Chief

Border Series

The Ward's Bride: Prequel Novella

The Thief's Countess ◆ The Lord's Captive

The Chief's Maiden ◆ The Scot's Secret

The Earl's Entanglement ◆ The Warrior's Queen

The Protector's Promise ◆ The Rogue's Redemption

The Guardian's Favor ◆ The Knight's Reward

Box Set 1 (Books 1-3) ◆ Box Set 2 (Books 4-6)

Kingdoms of Meria

The King's Commander ◆ My Highland Bride

Taken by the Elderman

Time Travel

Sexy Scot

Scandalous Scot

Falling for the Knight

Bloodwite (Contemporary PNR)

The Vampire's Temptation

The Immortal's Salvation ◆ The Hunter's Affection